The Black Box

The Black Box
stories

Mata Kastrisiou

Translated by Kostas Kaltsas

arb editions

AN IMPRINT OF
AK PRESS

The Black Box
Originally published by Εκδόσεις Ηριδανός as *Απορριμματοφόρα των έξι*

Anarchist Review of Books (https://anarchistreviewofbooks.org)
ARB Editions is an imprint of AK Press.

ISBN: 9781849356411
E-ISBN: 978184935648

AK Press
370 Ryan Ave. #100
Chico, CA 95973
United States
www.akpress.org

AK Press
33 Tower St
Edinburgh EH6 7BN
Scotland
www.akuk.com

The above addresses would be delighted to provide you with the latest AK Press distribution catalog, which features books, pamphlets, zines, and stylish apparel published and/or distributed by AK Press. Alternatively, visit our websites for the complete catalog, latest news, and secure ordering.

Cover design by Marc Lepson & Ben Durham
Cover photograph by yamasaki ko-ji (https://yamasakiko-ji.com). Used with permission.

Printed in the USA on acid-free paper

ARB Editions publishes incisive, expansive literary work that celebrates the radical imagination. Our titles are distinguished by the quality of their prose and their dedication to freedom. ARB Editions is a project of the *Anarchist Review of Books*, a print-only tabloid produced by an independent, international collective.

Μια λέξη είναι ο άνθρωπος
μια λέξη: «Τραγουδώντας»

To the memory of the poet Giorgos Blanas

Contents

The Black Box

stories

Editor's Note

Written in Greece during a period of economic and political upheaval, the stories in this slim volume draw upon the rich imagery of the Mediterranean, the Balkans, outer space, and a mythic, imaginary America.

The settings are tangible: an empty lot, the sea, a dumpster, a graveyard. But they are also out of time and place, unrecognizable. *The Black Box* is populated with intimate portraits—of neighbors, of lovers, of mothers—and archetypal abstractions—ghosts, mermaids, "photoelectric gods" who whisper in the reader's ear. In these shifts lies power and poetry.

Kastrisiou's language sits at the intersection of naturalism, surrealism, and abstraction. Deftly translated by Kostas Kaltsas, the writing retains its Greek character, at once emotionally probing, declaratory, and descriptive yet allusive and radically imaginative.

—ARB Editions

A House on Earth

Now night is falling, and we're all so tired that the strength has left our arms, the arms that are made to embrace, to lull someone to sleep, perhaps in some other place, some other time, not far from here. We fortified our city with the drawn-out languor of our songs and assumed our deaths would keep the profane and the complacent at bay.

By nightfall they will have breached our walls. Our children perch on the fence, war standards drawn with dirt on their faces, hurling rocks and rotten fruit. Young predators taking up their positions, toothless and weaponless, on the frontline of a timeless, futile battle. Our children. Skin and bones, and damaged mouths. You fell asleep early again, and besides, I know that nothing can wake you, not car horns, not music, not even my half-hearted calls for you to get out of bed. By morning it will all be over, and you'll be calmly afloat in your dreams, as sweet and serene as can be.

We were almost caught off guard. They tried to enter our city uninvited while we were holding a feast, and had taken off our shoes, and couldn't run, and we were late to our defenses, a few precious moments late. The feast, the likes of which aren't held anymore, spread out from one end of the city to the other. We'd laid colorful cloths on the long marble tables, and sat on the ground, in the tree's shade, and buried our palms in the dirt and felt a warmth as though we were holding the hands of our loved ones tight, whispering to them that we were there beside them. In this life people leave, whether in five years or in ten, so that one story can end and another can begin anew in its place.

We danced and sang, and all of us women wore a flower in our hair, at sunset your grandfather started singing an old, traditional tune, and tears poured down our faces, and we walked away, and only the children were left standing by his side, staring at him with their puzzled eyes as though they were staring at an ancient plane tree. When the song ended, they went back to their games, with their suntanned faces, back to the earthy summer, dusty, with strange air.

We were caught off guard. They entered our house uninvited, their clothes wrinkled, showing no respect. But we pitied them, and it's this compassion that makes us hold tightly to each other and together fortify our city walls. It's only a matter of minutes before a bulldozer is brought out to tear down our fence, we've decided in silent complicity that this battle will be hand to hand and last until this day is done and another day dawns for us.

It really is such a shame you fell asleep, for this was a great feast for our city. But how can I be mad at you? You grew tired, out all morning running around, playing, naked in your skin. And that sun, piercing your fingertips. Pinning your fingers down. I often think how different everything would be if we, too, lived with them, in the outside world, or in some other city with open borders or maybe a sea, or even some place the snow never stopped falling. Maybe I'd scold you all the time, who can say, fearing you'd get lost and not find your way home, fearing you'd catch a cold. Maybe you'd be such a bad student your teacher would summon me to your school to admonish me. Then again, maybe you'd be the best. What nonsense. Exiled here, we did at least spare our lives such painful worries, chronic damp phobias that come in winter like bedbugs under our mattresses. Outside our walls, innocence is circumscribed by the lines of a student notebook. I speak to you and leave gaps in my sentences in case you want to draw something in them. How foolish your mom is. How foolish.

I don't know how to tell the time, but I hear silence outside the walls and think it must be very late. Past midnight. Beside me some have fallen asleep, and I bite their hands to wake them, bite and kiss them even though I would very much like to let them lie like this for a while, calm, with lips half-closed and their breath a living thing touching my face, keeping me company. Besides, I'm used to being the one who stays awake.

When we came here years ago, we pleaded our way into our fair share of land. The earthquake had left us homeless, and all we wanted was a piece of ground where we could close our eyes and an empty plastic cup to seed with our memories, in the hope that one day they'd grow into the branches of something poisonous and smother us instantly. The mausoleums were, after all, as large as cellars. We only had to get used to lying down with someone else, sharing our sleep. It wasn't that hard, even though at first, at night, we were too embarrassed to scream lest we wake our companion in oblivion, and so we bit down on our own arms to stay silent, then spat out the blood, giving away the life that still dawned for us. Ten years now I've slept next to a frozen arm six inches long that clenched its fist stubbornly one night, stifling a quiet sob, a button of a tear, a pearl.

Behind the tombs we plant bulbs that grow into strange flowers, and our children grow up, play, run merrily among the trees and never fight among themselves, keep company to all the dead, give them their marbles, tend to their photographs with such care you'd think every face they touch was that of a dearest beloved. On Sundays, those outside our walls come visit and place small candles on the tombs, and the utter darkness grows lighter. Some of them stare with terror, fearing it's been so long, so eternally long, since they left their own families behind that only we remain to help them comb their hair in the morning and put on their Sunday best, help them disguise their sadness and old age. Yet they rush to leave before the sun has time to set, dusting off their clothes and looking mistrustfully around them as they walk, afraid of carrying off the faintest hint of sorrow. Few stay on till late and talk to us. They speak to us of life outside the walls, tell stories of old, laugh often, out loud. They look back at us fondly as they leave. They love us, just a little. They bring you candy, but I hide it from you, it's bad for your teeth and you have such a beautiful smile.

It's almost dawn, and I can hear cars approaching. At the sound of a gunshot everyone next to me was startled awake, went back to bracing the walls. The cries from beyond them grow more savage, synchronized, mechanical, the crackle and static of an out-of-tune station. Woe to those who claimed it's we who disturb the dead. Already a part of our fence has collapsed and someone's jumped through it. My screams are not enough, my mouth is not enough, my hands, I'll cut them off, what good are they, can hold on to nothing, protect nothing. Our people are retreating as the gunfire grows heavier. Where can I go, inside which tomb can I hide? All available space taken up by the dead in their hundreds, fighting to get out, crawling over each other's backs, jostling, and I have no arms to embrace them with and quiet them down. Don't wake up now, don't see, don't feel. Rest peacefully asleep, my child, I'll remain here with you, though I might be the only one, for where would I go, where would I live? No matter how big the house I'm given not even my head will fit inside, at night it will grow huge and seek you out, reach for the walls, press up against them, tear them down.

Our forts have collapsed and so have our walls, making a muffled sound as though in pain. We crawl on all fours and the outside world with its guns and cars invades the pedestrian walkway, contaminating it. Marble collapses and breaks to pieces on our faces, take care my child, don't you die a second time, don't be killed, put the sky over your head and protect yourself, and let me hold the pillars and the stones, let me be the one to blame for not building you a house solid enough that not even death could tear it down. And not knowing, still, and always staying up at night, in case you ever want to tell me, my boy, only if you want to, whether, trapped down there in the wreckage of a life that wasn't spared, whether you felt pain or whether you hummed under your breath that nursery rhyme about Papa Rabbit and his six bunnies and one kid goat, the one he fed carrots to so it would grow up just like his other children and learn to wiggle its ears and its pink nose and nibble its food with its little teeth and be smart and beautiful and clean.

The sun is high again, two hands covered in filth are dragging me out of my city. The police gather up our clothes and crockery, and not a single god in the sky to rain down fire to burn us bright in our tears. I'm pushed and kicked, and it was only a feast, a small, quiet feast, and I left gaps between the words for you to fill if you ever wanted to. With the last of my might I hold on to a handful of dirt, and as they're pulling me out of you, away from you, I begin to chew and chew it and swallow it with my saliva and my tears and think I can hear you whisper from inside your square little house, whisper and walk in your sleep. Stay in your bed, and don't get up, it's late, it's very late, the sun's turned dark, the sun's turned black, it's night, the deepest, thickest night, don't get up, your mama is watching over you, how foolish your mom is, how foolish.

They've got us on some upper floor, way up high, all crammed together. Near the top of a high-rise. They even gave us blankets. In summertime. Through its floor-to-ceiling windows I can make out, far away, two cities, one by the sea, one with open borders where the snow never stops falling. Place is a concept even more abstract than death.

And now, my child, how can I part with you.

Garbage Trucks at 6 am

My mother's face smelled of the sea. I no longer recall her form. It's been centuries. Her body must lie buried somewhere, and maybe one day all the disconsolate, yearning to be held, will find it by its odor, unearth it, and lose themselves in oceanic depths and summer afternoons. The memory that bodies give off is stronger than that of love.

I sought nothing more than warm sleep. Next to the remnants of days and the clutter of people. At night I climbed up to my little green house, a barefoot cat with its ears bloodied, and until sleep came I made up stories about children's ruined shoes and rotten apples. Soon I fell asleep. The silence of the garbage is unbearable at night, when all falls quiet. Sometimes I slid my bin on its little wheels along wide avenues and left my roof open—the sky revealing itself to me full of stars.

I no longer have hands. Now I'll have to climb up using my teeth. The street's strays will bark at me and mob me in the dark. No one comes near me because I reek. If anyone dared stand by me for a few minutes I would whisper that once upon a time, my hair was bleached white and smelled of cedar, and lilies bloomed in my hands.

New Year's Day was dawning, and I closed my eyes, curled up and quiet. I lay on festive wreaths, and the sequin of a broken bauble nicked my cheek. The angels came down from the Christmas tree and covered me, the only ones who could stand the smell washing up on the shores of my eyes. I woke to noise and pain without end. At first I thought it was the cold. Then out of my mouth fell orange peels and stories from the back issues of the papers. A trial, a robbery, a suicide. The thirty-fourth suicide. My bones crushed, I weighed nothing now, sinking into slow, eternal immobility in the thick depths of foul sensations and waste. The new year found me limbless.

If you can see me, Mother, wrap your disfigured child in a warm wool blanket, and lay it atop the trash pile. I'll give off something of the aura of the seashore, supervise the recycling process of day and night. When it rains, the whole city will be in the thrall of a heavy scent. "We live in wild and bloody times," they'll say. People will shut their windows and mutter obscenities. Out in the streets, the garbage trucks, in those loneliest hours of the day, will veer off course and cross paths with ambulances and comets.

Now I can no longer sleep. My head floats atop broken shoulders. My hope is in death. When I meet you, I'll be freshly bathed and clean. We'll wear our Sunday finest, there'll be a feast.

The Blue Comet

When the sky decides to rain, the rain always comes at 7:25 in the morning, the time, that is, when I leave the house and start walking to school. Grandma gives me a brown umbrella, but it's embarrassing to carry because it's a woman's umbrella, and half busted. So, I get there soaking wet and shake the water off me and onto my sweetest classmate shouting, "Booooo! I'm the God of Thunder!" and she says I'm being silly and walks out of the classroom with a mocking laugh. Today is one of those days, its color is electric blue and the schoolyard empty. At the window, I stick my face to the glass and imagine that if I were Blue, the Channel 7 cartoon legend, I could break it with a single glance, fly over the building, and stop the rain. Blue has died and risen four times in all these years we've been watching the show. He is immortal, as all heroes are. It occurs to me that, though he's unrecognizable when out and about as his real self, if he happened to be in a bank with robbers bursting through the door, he'd rip off his suit to reveal his fluorescent costume, and everyone would exclaim, "Oh my God! It's Blue!" and he'd save his city from certain doom.

It's almost noon, and the raindrops are still coming down so hard I'm starting to think the water will never leave our yard, and by the time the sun comes out the school will have turned into a giant lake, and December will find us playing and splashing around, happy in our mottled swimsuits. There's no class when it rains, the teachers are always late, and so for at least the whole first period we take turns drying our shoes on the rusty radiators in the hallways. It seems to me that such overcast days give us all an opportunity to sit quietly at our desks for a while and just listen to the sound of raindrops striking the concrete out in the yard, where on sunny mornings we play ball and hide-and-seek, where we fall and skin our knees before we come home stained and bloodied.

Our town is small and dusty. In winter, the edges of the streets vanish, and we live within an endless grey. Our house is close to the swamp, and so my fingers always feel sticky, and sometimes I think I see little green specks on my skin. On Sundays, Grandma hands us a fish net and teaches us how to strangle the big frogs with our bare hands and how to find treasures in the swamp water. Grandma is a round shadow. She sits at the table shelling seeds with her teeth, discarding the shells and collecting the dozens of little spheres that will later fill our bellies in a big tub. We call her Old Lady Shady and make up little songs about her and laugh, but deep down we love her dearly, she's been taking it upon herself for years now to bake us cakes on our birthdays and wake us up in the morning for school. I don't think the Blue Comet would be all that happy if he lived in our home, since nothing extraordinary ever happens in our town nor has anyone ever tried to poison any of us with some malodorous toxic compound.

Around our town roam dozens of bugs and lizards, and I collect the strangest in a big jar I place high above my bed. Once, attempting to reach it, my sister knocked it down and the room was filled with strange, dazed little creatures stumbling into the corners of all the furniture. Then Grandma walked in and one by one killed them all with her gun. That certainly didn't curb my interest in lizards, even though since then they've been slowly disappearing from the area. I'm sure Grandma chased them away. Old Lady Shady Mommy.

Most people in our town own guns, and that's because when the weather clears, they go out hunting small birds, returning with them as trophies. I never eat them. When Dad isn't tired, he wakes me up early on Saturday mornings, teaches me to aim from a distance. We bring my best friend Ray along, but I always beat him at target practice. It never seems to truly bother him. Besides, he looks up to me, I'm six whole months older. Target practice is a fun game considering I could grow up to be the rusty-barreled hero in whose honor Channel 7 will screen a new cartoon. It even occurs to me it'd be nice if the studio invited me to lend the cartoon my voice, but only if my vocal cords stop embarrassing me with all their croaking and squeaking and cacophonous animal sounds.

And so, every day seems as still as the swamp outside our house. I'm already halfway through elementary school, and I still can't make my way through a sentence without faltering two or three times. During class I chew on my pencil and doodle chase sequences and spaceships full of all my classmates all over the margins of my book's pages. The girls too. So, when the teacher asks me a question, I snap awake and yell, "WHAT?" even though Mom would counsel us to always say, "EXCUSE ME?" instead of "WHAT?" My hope is that, what with how early school starts every morning, everyone realizes how sleepy we are and forgives us our trespasses.

It all began on November 27, after the credits rolled on the Sunday morning cartoons an ad came on: X-Cheese cheese puffs were launching a huge contest with ten winners who'd each receive a plane ticket to accompany Blue Comet to the premiere of the first movie about his exploits. According to the ad, inside ten out of thousands and thousands of bags of cheese puffs were the lucky fluorescent stickers that meant you'd won.

I stopped saving money for a soccer ball. I also stopped buying Grandma those vanilla hard candies she loved every Friday. Not only did I buy ten bags of cheese puffs a day, I also felt horribly obligated to eat them all or else I'd be a thief and wimp. Soon I gathered that all my classmates had been doing the same because every five minutes or so someone would ask the teacher permission to go to the bathroom, and we all had this pale-yellow dust all over our faces and a bacon-and-baked-potato outline on our teeth.

The mood at school took a strange turn. We'd look at each other funny and keep our hands in our pockets. After class, none of us were in the mood for soccer, we all ran home eager to turn on the TV, we all knew the ad by heart, and our parents couldn't stand us anymore. What's more, we'd given up on girls, who could never fathom some of our plans. We had a whole world to save while they busied themselves with kitchenware and jewelry. At night we had trouble sleeping, in the grip of this tremendous anxiety that when we woke in the morning our classmate at the next desk over would announce he'd found the lucky bag. We began playing marbles, gambling with what little money we had in hope we'd be able to buy more cheese puffs. Our neighborhood shopkeepers knew who we were by now and would greet us with mocking smiles whenever they saw us, the know-it-alls, as though they had the slightest clue what it meant to be Blue. I grew suspicious of even these sad, fat-assed shopkeepers, who'd wasted their entire lives stuck in the same muddy town while we were getting ready to blast off to the farthest reaches of the galaxy in our fluorescent costumes. I thought they'd cut a secret deal with the manufacturing plant and Blue himself to advertise the product, to sell us as many bags as they could and in return receive the lucky sticker as a gift and get to travel in the company of the legend that haunted our dreams. No one should trust anyone, not anymore.

Disaster struck on a Friday immediately after first recess. It was the last day of school before the holidays, and our teacher, right after reaching the end of the chapter on the troposphere, handed out little Christmas presents for everyone. Us boys got model airplanes and car kits while the girls got these tiny doll babies with a hollow stomach that you could feed milk or water. One day I'll be a grown-up, and I still won't get this obsession girls have with feeding imaginary babies. I mean, here they are, still peeing their pants from time to time, thinking themselves capable of nursing as much as a plastic doll. Last summer my sister fed boiling milk to one of these dolls, an old one belonging to our grandma, causing its stomach to melt and the doll to spew its guts. Sweetened milk all over our living room, and the doll left with its belly gaping and its blond hair wet and mushed flat. Anyway, these were the kinds of gifts our teacher handed out, but she'd saved the best for last. She'd had the brilliant idea of giving each desk one bag of cheese puffs, stressing that we'd already eaten too many of these for her to hand us each a full bag and that eating such disgusting things went against everything she stood for, but, not wanting us to think she didn't feel for us, she'd gone against her beliefs to offer us this last small gift. That was more or less what she said before handing out the bags. I took the bag in my hands, and Ray, whom I'd sat with since the first grade, asked me to open it because his hands were shaking. I tore it open it a little begrudgingly. Outside it was already drizzling, and the clouds had drifted down almost as low as the green hoop in our basketball court. We were halfway through the bag when my greasy hand picked out something that didn't feel like a cheese puff. I shut my eyes and for one moment saw myself in Blue's arms, flying over our rickety school, our stupid town. I pulled my hand out of the bag, looked inside my palm and saw an edge of fluorescent paper poking out of the cheesy mess. "Ray," I said, "Ray, I think we won." I pulled out the piece of paper, blew off the cheesy crumbs, and laid it on the desk. It was square and prettier than I'd imagined. It read: *Young friend, I'd be honored to take you with me on a journey across the skies. Be brave.* It was signed, *Blue.*

I grabbed Ray, who was sniffling with joy, and we ran out of the classroom. We ducked inside the boys' toilets, latching the cubicle door behind us. We took turns holding the increasingly crumpled piece of smooth, glossy paper. We were considering skipping music class to call the listed number and give our names as soon as possible, just in case we didn't make it in time, and the plane left without us. I'd decided long ago that if I won, I'd take my new soccer boots with me plus my big poster of Blue for him to sign. It would be my first time on a plane, the first time I set foot outside the borders of our town. Maybe if I asked the pilot would let me sit on his lap and put on his big headphones. The flight attendant would give me the mic, and I'd start singing the TV show's theme song and get the whole plane going: "A universe full of wonder and might, a hero emerges, a beacon of light. Blue

Comet, the name that echoes through space, a champion of justice that evil can't face!" Suddenly, gripped with horror, I opened my eyes and examined the palm clenching the piece of paper. "Ray," I said, "The sticker is meant for one person. There's only one seat."

We walked out of the toilets without saying another word. Outside, half the school was gathered waiting for us, and the yard was given over to an immense silence. A pigeon was pecking at cheese puff crumbs on the dirty concrete, and the rain was coming down in earnest. We didn't speak. Just looked at everyone for a moment or two, dumbfounded, then left. Some things really are just between friends.

I came home soaking wet and went to my room, closing the door behind me. I didn't even feel like bothering with the solitary lizard still alive inside the glass jar. Grandma asked me if I wanted cheese croquettes for lunch, and at their mere mention I ran to the bathroom and threw up a hundred bags of X-Cheese, crying and sobbing all the while. I wished that Christmas had never come. I fell into bed and imagined an entire colony of cheese puffs had grown inside my stomach and were even now plotting my extermination. Not an hour passed before I heard the yard gate slam open. Here came Ray, with a stupid beanie on his head. He said, "Man, don't worry about it, we're really very lucky either way. But one of us has to go. Us finding the sticker is the greatest thing that's ever happened in this shithole of a town." I gave him a loving little shove. I never expected him to be this brave. His peculiar purple eyes lit up with joy. "We'll put it up as the prize for our Sunday game," he went on. "We'll set up our usual team hide-and-seek game, and whoever wins—it'll be well deserved. We're grown men, after all." He closed the yard gate behind him and set off for home, and I was left there staring at him from a distance as he walked away with something almost like a skip to his step, kicking the stones in his way and mumbling to himself. We would meet Sunday 5 pm at the old garbage dump. He was my best friend.

The old garbage dump is frequently chosen as our playground

for the thousands of treasures it has to offer. You can come across old steering wheels, torn-up comic books, deflated balloons, all mixed in with rotten fruit and beer bottles. Most of the garbage has been taken away by now, but two or three hill-sized piles remain to give the place its special air of solemnity. Approaching our meeting point, I was happy. I almost didn't care anymore. I'd decided that whatever would be would be and that, for the love of God, we'd thrown away all our money on this stupid thing, one way or another it had to end. I got there first, walked about the place once, found a red marble lying around, and put it in my pocket. Soon the rest of them arrived. Every boy in my class. We quickly split up into two teams and were ready to go. We agreed no one would cheat, no one would peek, no one would steal a glance, Ray and I shook hands, and we buried the sticker under an old rusty fridge. It was time.

It was, in truth, a really fun game, we were still playing over two hours later with the score tied. We'd almost forgotten about the prize. The girls had started to gather around us. We felt awfully strong. It was my turn to be it. I counted out loud and went looking. I moved slowly, making the opposing team even more anxious, walked around the spot we call the Car Graveyard and examined with exaggerated interest a flat tire lying on the ground with weeds growing out of the hole in its middle. Suddenly, Lee came running at top speed from behind the tallest hill, and I saw him approaching home base, about to reach safety and cost me the round. Blue appeared in front of me, and I thought I heard him say something. I set off running. I almost flew. At the risk of losing sight of Lee, I opted to go around the back route to make up some time. Mere seconds later we came upon each other, a stone's throw away from home base. I couldn't feel my legs. I saw Ray step out of his hiding place and stare at us, stunned and helpless. The girls had ceased their stupid giggling. I launched myself forward and landed on home base one step ahead of Lee, and yelled, "Out, Lee! You're out!"

They all came out of their hiding places, looking terrible. We all knew there was just one round to go. I realized I only had one shoe on, and my clothes were a mess. If only we could pull it off . . . If only my team could hold on. . . . In that moment I felt that last round was nothing like the hundreds of games we'd played up till then. I realized that if I lost there'd be nothing left for me to look forward to in this shitty town, and I'd have to wait until I finished elementary school and was given a bicycle I could ride to get away from all those bored-stiff, pig-faced, idiot shopkeepers in my neighborhood. It was Ray's turn to be it.

He turned his back to us and started counting. I ran far away, hiding behind the rusty fridge we'd buried the sticker under. Not in a million years would it occur to Ray to look for me there. Just as he was nearing the end of his count and crying out "Ready or not, here I come!" no more than a second before he came out seeking, I saw O'Malley out of the corner of my eye trying to stuff himself inside a cardboard box. He was the chubbiest and slowest of us all, and he was on my team. I jumped out of my hiding place and grabbed him and the box he'd put over his head. I shoved him behind the fridge and before I could tuck his flabby gut away, Ray was already heading straight for us as though he knew. He came within spitting distance. And saw O'Malley's gut sticking out. Perhaps it was me he saw first, but I'll never get a chance to ask. Some things really are just between friends. "O'Malley! I see you, O'Malley!" he called out, and started backing away. My whole team came out of hiding, running toward home base. I was furious, my fists were clenched, the sticker in one of them, tears streaming from my eyes. That's when I called out, "Ray! It's not right, and you know it! He wasn't done hiding!" He paid me no mind, and I started to bray. A flock of blackbirds took flight and flew away. "He's the fattest of us all, it's not fair, you knew he didn't stand a chance! Ray! You asshole! Stop right there!" But Ray wouldn't listen. I stopped running and started throwing rocks at him, screaming, "Ray, goddammit! Goddammit, I'll never speak to you again, you moron! I'll never hang out with you again!" I was throwing rocks and crying and wishing the ground of the dump would split open and swallow me whole, so I'd never again have to lay eyes on our stingy teacher or those lizards or the swamp or anything at all. "Ray!" I screamed, "Ray, you dumbass, you really think Blue wants anything to do with wimps like you, you thieving son of a bitch?" and threw a rock at him as hard as I could. Ray turned around, looked at me with those purple eyes of his, and collapsed in the dirt.

Everyone stopped running, both out of breath and holding their breath. I unclenched my fists and saw my sweat had eaten away at the sticker I'd been squeezing all this time. Slowly, I approached Ray. Now both my shoes were gone. I stood next to him. He was lying on his back, my rock had hit him in the head. A small pool of blood was forming among the garbage and muddy water. I heard very soft crying coming from the spot where the girls were gathered. I leaned over him and looked. His upper lip was covered in a yellow mustache of cheese-puff dust. You're out, Ray. We're all out.

We got to the end of the fourth grade. Learned about the stratosphere and the ionosphere and all the atmospheres. But nowhere in the entire book was there anything written about the thick fog that descends over our town on most winter days. The Blue Comet movie premiered in New York in mid-August. I didn't turn on the TV to watch. But I'm sure that Ray, my best friend Ray, made the trip seated next to the pilot and is now Blue's Secret Agent Number One. I see him in his huge beanie that always hangs over his eyes, leading a flock of birds towards the horizon. Not like our own raucous birds: He's leading these orange pelicans on an important mission to a hidden galaxy. He flies high, over our stupid town, hovering among plastic model cars and thousands of bags of pickle-flavored cheese puffs, earnestly overseeing millions of violet explosions in a bright sky all his own.

PS

He stood before a hypnotic, photoelectric god. His memory was gone, but he held on to a fleeting image of advertisements and Saturday morning cartoons. His mother a lottery hostess on TV. Blonde and worn down. When he was born, she gave him a blessing and left for the west.

The god barely recognized the boy. After all, he'd swallowed fistfuls of pills, and the forms surrounding him looked almost spectral. The boy wore a pair of rusty fins for wings and carried torn-up comic books tucked under his armpit. Nebulae and shooting stars were projected on multiple screens around the room. The music was electric, and they were surrounded by hatching dinosaurs, Amazons, and girls from school yearbooks.

God said, "It's quite the crazy day you picked to show up. Dawn's taking her time."

Outside the window, snow was falling and with it bits of burnt photographs.

The boy said, "I get sad when comets crash into the galaxy and die."

An Amazon painted blue all over sparkled, stopped her dancing and approached him. She gave him a box of flat-pack universes.

Every boy has some sorrow or other under the lips, every boy has his own constellation.

Asteroid 623 Chimera, 57 Mnemosyne

A.

On Asteroid 623 the weather is icy. The bottle of modafinil on the metal table is almost empty and a 3D notice floating over the cap is reminding him it needs refilling. The man has leaned slightly forward and is carefully disconnecting the cable that links the computer to the microchip embedded in his left wrist. It's time for his evening meal.

"Gloria! My dinner!" he shouts hoarsely, and she appears holding a tray bearing a green pill and a glass filled with blue liquid. She blinks affectionately, her electronic voice radiating out to infinity—a combination of coded tones and bright repeating cyclical waves directed at the man. "Your dinner, Joe." Having made sure the man has taken the pill, she places the glass back on the tray, then stands for a moment beside him and tenderly caresses his back. She thinks he looks sad tonight. He welcomes the caress, and Gloria increases and decreases the intensity of her touch based on his reactions to her movements. Her artificial skin functions flawlessly, her sense of touch achieved with absolute precision. "Goodnight, Joe," she announces, and reading in the man's thoughts a desire for solitude, she rolls noiselessly out of the room.

Her exit generates a certain electricity in the space around him that the man perceives as a wet film covering his eyes, preventing him from focusing on the room's objects. When he rises from the chair, his vision returns, and he calmly walks over to the window. It was exactly five years ago, on a night as cold as tonight, the night of his daughter's seventh birthday, that he settled on 623. Now, as far as the eye can see: aerodynamic homes and aluminum tracks. Neon and exploding stars. God-planets, separated by a universe decaying by the day, sprinkling its dust over the galaxies. Traces of that dust landing daily on the man's hair, which turns grey, then white. A beautiful young man with crushed stars in his hair.

He's roused from his sad indolence by a computer signal about some distant asteroid named 57. There's a celebration on it tonight, and small rockets are launched into the sky to break into thousands of flaming pieces. From so great a distance they look to the man like colorful balloons and streamers and pink heart-shaped cookies and lollipops and little striped pennants. He suddenly feels the vertigo of infinity, but for a moment at least, a calmness comes over him. Gloria is in the next room, if he needs her, he'll call out, and she'll take him in her arms and hold tight with those wired muscles and whisper the comforting words stored in her software.

So, the man surrenders to the feeling of his neighbors' celebration, which still reminds him of something he can't place. Familiar songs, lost in overwritten memory, radiate through the galaxy, overwhelming the man. Prophetic in their day, their melodies by now outdated. But 57 is too far away, and the music is fading, and the man needs to hear it, he'd been told of that sense of absolute cold that invades the body, especially at night, the sense that can't be banished by lighting small candles, lighting fires, torching the universe, yet the man hadn't believed what he'd been told. And it's infinitely short and infinitely long, the time you have to think, when you find yourself in darkness so thick it looks now like black water, now like a solid square box, utterly unmoving and immovable, hard and cold as steel. And so, the man decides to do what three years ago would have never even crossed his mind. He decides to turn back, and look, recalling that myth about Eurydice he read to his daughter at bedtime, only this Eurydice wears a suit of steel, and even her eyes don't show, and what words of love she has to share are not songs, not sobs but equations and metals and megabytes and explosions.

In one abrupt motion he grabs his suit and puts it on and attaches its multicolored wires to the emergency exit. The great gate slowly opens, and the sound reaches his ears more distinct, more recognizable. And the man begins to swim around the room or perhaps dance lazily, an uninvited guest in his neighbors' celebration. But the wires are only long enough for a few dance moves, and he wants to turn them into a transparent belt that will fix him to the celebration's center. Which is why he pulls at the wires. And the wires in turn pull him back. And now this turns into a tug-of-war, with the small silver wires fighting to keep him inside the room. And the time to think about the losses entailed in such a defeat is infinitely short and infinitely long, and so the man pulls hard on the taut wires. Right away, the computer sounds a repeating alarm as emergency lights flash along the aluminum track. And he can no longer close the gate. The room's door abruptly seals itself, and the man turns around, terrified. "Gloria!" he calls out, but his voice cracks and floats off into space and is only registered by the computer, a small, weak signal, its range zero. Through the window he makes out a multicolored festive rocket heading toward him at tremendous speed. With gigabytes of music and brilliance flowing through his cables, he stands there observing the rocket. Seconds before the security system stops working, the man turns to the gate and, with all his senses heightened, sees the missile come closer and closer and finally stab him right between the eyes, scattering into each pupil thousands of tiny, infinity-confirming, vertigo-negating stars. Infinity inside something as familiar as a melody misplaced in stacks of back-ups, in blurry images projected one after another on the steel wall with its automatic illumination, the wall by the sealed security door, behind Gloria, through Gloria, Gloria waiting, feelings of fear activated, for Joe to survive this and take her along on his journey to the stars.

With a thud, the man drops dead on the aluminum track.

B.

Hearing the sound, Gloria calls out from the next room, "Joe, could you please turn down the TV?"

Gloria stands at the kitchen sink in her floral robe, clearing leftovers of this evening's dinner, scrubbing the dishes one after another under the hot tap. The kitchen is small, with colorful tiles lining the front of the wooden counter and stacked jars of spices on the shelf. An old-timey show is on the radio, and Gloria knows that any moment now the host will get to her request. This happens every Wednesday night, Gloria calls the station without giving them her real name, which sounds to her insipid, then waits, impatience mounting, for them to play her song. Around this time, Joe is lying on the living room sofa watching TV with his feet propped up on the low coffee table. The sofa's a two-seater, its diamonds-and-circles upholstery frayed and fading. The house fading with it. There's no nursery. Neither pink nor blue. Damp spreads from the ceiling when it rains, and the hallway tiling is all cracks and stains. When the house sinks, Gloria is certain it will take Joe with it. She'll save herself by climbing onto the roof, holding on to the TV antenna and communicating with a distant star.

Gloria doesn't know what ingredient turned the recipe of her marriage bitter. As for tonight, she wishes something would change. Not for long. Just for a little while. Fat from their boiled fish floats in the sink, and she reaches in with a hand sheathed in a yellow rubber glove to pull the plug. A sharp bone lodged in the drain pricks and bloodies her finger. Blood covers the glove, and she stands still over the sink, watching the stain grow and spread.

"Joe, didn't you hear me? How much longer do I need to keep asking you to turn the volume down . . ." she's saying as she comes through the kitchen door and finds the man unconscious, lying in a heap on the living room floor. Gloria doesn't bend over him, isn't frightened, doesn't draw back. She doesn't call out, doesn't reach for the phone, doesn't clamp a hand over her mouth, doesn't wonder, nor is she sure. Her request comes on the radio: "To my dear friend Stella." Gloria smiles. "Stella" is Italian for "star," she remembers this from school, from some poem or other. She sits calmly on the diamonds-and-circles sofa, peeling an orange from the fruit bowl, its aroma sweet in her nostrils. She eats staring at the TV as if in a trance as the end credits of a documentary titled *Asteroid 623 Chimera, 57 Mnemosyne* roll down the screen.

The night is dressed formally. Technicolor signs and the playful horns of sports cars, furs, skyscrapers, highways, lipstick, music, kisses. Gloria knows nothing of the night. She stares, enchanted, and often bumps into people who give her curious, inquiring looks. Yet she has long been prepared for tonight. She hasn't gone out partying in years, and no one could hold it against her were she to overdo it with her outfit or makeup, not tonight. But Gloria knows. And she's a beautiful woman. Not what you'd objectively call a beauty—if you saw her in a penthouse duplex, you'd peg her as a nondescript forty-five year old, haggard and melancholy. What's happening is that Gloria is subtly giving herself over to her circumstances and the times and letting them transform her. So that anyone who'd happened to run into her in the supermarket or drugstore would not recognize her, not tonight. She's waiting for the light to turn green, more eagerly than she's waited for anything her whole life. Perhaps because, for years now, when she imagined this night, everything on the other side of this particular street was lit up differently. And Gloria knows no other light but the icy glare of the TV screen. And the light turns green.

Joe stood up in a daze and almost fell back onto the sofa. His head felt heavy, and it took a few seconds for him to realize where he was and what had happened. On the coffee table there was a bowl full of oranges, the TV was on Channel 7, and in the house a quiet reigned, different than the kind he was used to. He got up slowly and went to the kitchen. He left the tap running and filled his glass until it overflowed, and water started dripping down the cabinet and onto the tiles. Gloria's narrow little kitchen a pool of stagnant water.

Joe loves Gloria, especially come summer. She wears an enormous hat, sits in the shade, and stares at the young people on the beach in complete surrender to the fluidity of the afternoon. Joe loves Gloria, especially when she sleeps. She breathes softly, her cheeks pulled into a smile. In her dreams, she wears a backpack and speeds away on an old motorbike, denying the present version of her life as the only one possible. Joe watches her roll lightly to one side in her sleep and tries to figure out which movie character she reminds him of. A character in a wide colorful skirt with a narrow waistband, a mouth that's vivid red. He gets up from the sofa, slouches over to the TV and turns it off, opens the front door and walks out.

Gloria floats inside a universe made of her own small sensations, incubated for years inside a dank cabinet. She doesn't know precisely how she should stand, but the man's skin feels familiar, a good fit for her own, and if she shifts her gaze a little higher, what she'll see up above is a fluorescent green, strangely rectangular moon. Finite and uneven ground she could cover in just a few hours, if she wanted to—crawling like a baby on all fours, exploring his skin with her knees and tongue—the taste of lipstick on her lips and drops of sweat shining in the darkness like those little twinkling stars, those drifters through space. From neck to shoulder to the joints of the pelvis and the hollows behind the knees, curves and sinuous runways, and movement sometimes languid, free of gravity, sometimes like a violent forced landing. She pushes the man's body deep inside. Nothing bloodier than that, nothing deeper. She'd like to rip her belly open, take in the whole of him, swallow him up in fiery heat. And at the highest point of the dome she was taught was the sky, thousands of tiny stars break into droplets of sweat and tears, and yet others rush toward the watery blue planet she was taught was the Earth, and she wishes they would crash into it and in a single, solitary moment, obliterate it.

Gloria gets out of the minivan parked on the side of the street with a blurry image in her mind's eye of the man having fallen asleep. She counts back years to a summer, an old motorbike, the dirt of a county road, the possibility of a life that could have been a different one. The exit light on the roof of the car flickers for a few seconds, the green moon short-circuits and goes out, plunging everything into darkness.

It was past three when Gloria unlocked the door. As soon as she entered the hall, she felt an unexpected coldness envelope her. She glanced in the mirror, made a funny face, and walked into the living room expecting to find Joe's body still lying on the floor. With the bright TV screen off, the whole house was bathed in an eerie darkness, and Gloria wondered, actually wondered, if what she'd seen earlier had been an illusion borne of fatigue and went searching for Joe in the kitchen, then the bedroom. Then she came back and sat on the couch, counted the diamonds, counted the circles, scooched over, lay down, stretched, curled into a ball. Hours went by this way. The night whose arrival she'd spent years anticipating had now passed, and this feeling was familiar to her. There was nothing emptier than it. Than this. She got off the couch and lit a cigarette. It was a strange, melancholy thing, Gloria's awkward smoking. In her red lipstick and colorful skirt, she probably looks like a character in a movie, but she hasn't seen enough movies to say for sure. She smiled and blew smoke out through her nostrils. When the house sinks, it'll drag Joe down with it.

It was six am with Gloria at the window, one of those freezing-cold winters, the two-bedroom apartment on the top floor, a home with neither pink nor blue, and somewhere else a Stella or Judith or Laura was pulling up her slip in the black-and-white dawn. Gloria turned to see an airplane high above, carving out its slow course through the sky, flying into clouds then out again. That's when the woman wished with all her heart that the galaxy would empty out, that in an instant all the stars and the little wishes each carried would be gone, and all that would be left would be this sad sky above, to hold, to cover, to protect and keep us.

Alexander and the Mermaid

Moray's brother, weever's son, the bronze votive you were offered at birth was rusted by the sea, your teeth, left in steel-hard rock, crushed between them in an instant; then, no more poison, no more bite, you buried yourself under the sand.

Too late, my dear. You ascended too late, took in breath too late. The summer fish escaped and will outlive you. But it will remember you, the only one to see the strange markings on its tail. Its azure. Its orange.

I know you dove in after the mermaid. To ask her how it is that she's still alive. But she'd long since given up on both the sea bottom and her quandaries. Alexander is dead, his body decaying on the shore. Thousands of small crabs vacate it—prey for the seagulls.

The mermaid evolved as a species, she now wears heels and goes around the harbor shops asking if anyone has coke to spare. But the sailors of her day went down with their ships years ago, and their pipes lay smoking in the sea, and their laughter thunders down below.

Forgotten harbor queen, she mourns her braggart of a brother.

The day would come when you would drown. There is in all our summers a moment we're fated not to surface.

And the beaches will empty of people. And autumn will come. And the leaves of the trees will drift from the forests and quilt the surface of the sea. Breathing, a process first introduced at our birth that we've yet to master.

Every June I swim out to open water, and when it grows dark, I see you, out between two islands, black and blue. A tiny fish escapes your lips, feeding off your saliva to survive.

Our castles were besieged and sacked. I'm out digging wells to start the story over. To find water. I dig my nails in the sand, my bucket fills with seaweed and stones, my toy shovel bends out of shape, catches against a horse's skull, my hands black with oil. No one on the beach. The chill of early autumn, children in cardigans in the squares. And as I watch the lights come on across the water, the ships cut through the sea—brave, patient voyagers—I think of you rising naked out of the water and feel a tremendous urge to eat your eyes, the moistness of your eyes.

The memory of you is iodine red, the days go by like a course of antibiotics.

Tonight, I'll drown angry. For not seizing your lips to numb them with my sharp kisses.

In my dreams, the deities of the sea worship at your feet, and I don't know their names to thank them. And your barnacled mouth can't tell me.

We only ever loved one mermaid, and she betrayed us. And we've drunk so much seawater for her sake since we were babies. We carry inside us a small seabed of coral and rusty anchors that pierce our stomachs, bleed them out.

Now I'm out searching for any little bastard, dusky harbor children the mermaid might have popped out, to take to our bed for just one night. Let them caress you with their tails. You'll be more alive than ever.

It's only a matter of time before you won't be able to ascend.

Hey you, sailor, with your cloud-white sail,
who keeps the secrets in the old-time tale
Answer me please
I'm on my knees

brave Alexander have you seen,
astride the horse in his all-light skin
sword in his hand slashing at the waves,
go under and drown, rise up from the graves,
marry the sea, kiss sweet his bride,
maps of the world in her eyes open wide
beseech her, tell him he's alive.

Moray's brother, weever's son, we'll meet again one day. Jump over the fires on St. John's. Those love-affair summers are the greatest. Our memory is June and July and August.

My Scorpio, my summer constellation, Cygnus, how many millions of lightyears away shall we meet again?

I'll lie awake till dawn to watch you cross the Tigris, the Euphrates, and the Ganges, to dismount your horse on my terrace by the pot of basil. You'll empty your pockets of all their sand and offer me your eyes, unripe cherries for me to devour. Behind us the sea will dawn, we'll enter it sightless, swim through our summer, come out made whole on winter's shore.

Easter Week

Out on the highways of our strife the midday hour arrives quietly, so quietly we don't even hear it in our sleep and are eventually awakened by a strange sensation of fire. A sly languor spreads over drivers' faces, and the asphalt steams and whatever is buried underneath fights to rise to the surface, breaking the icy mixture of tar with a series of small monotonous blows. There are no trees by the asphalt, no other identifying marker. One bend is no different than the next, there is no hint of safety. Always you must drive with someone next to you, someone to talk you into wakefulness. At night, the bright ramps dazzle, twinkling stars caged in iron boxes. If, seduced by their beauty, you pursue them, the universe will reveal itself to you, eternal and irrevocable.

The woman with the baby bump and dappled dress walks by the side of the road, yet no car pulls over to pick her up. There's only whistling and leering glances from monstrous rigs. Immigrant of an age that is always coming and forever passing by, the woman, in her old-fashioned robe, is only seeking a place to give birth. Each year her belly is rounder, the babies in her arms fewer.

Every home hides a dead child of its own, tucked away, as a rule, in a cupboard alongside the good china. There it sits, peaceful and quiet, only waking up at night to bite down on the tea saucers and fill its mouth with blood.

Her children don't know the difference between a pine and a willow; their dream's horizon is an air shaft and a city in a trance. They can recite by heart bus routes and science volumes, but to recognize a wild rosebush—they're sorry but they can't. Why would you banish them now, then, just because they can't get their fingers to adapt to picking up a lily? Why feed them tinctures and powders to make them sleep? Give them the shade of a tree. And running water. And a canyon. If you can.

It's late afternoon when the woman finally reaches the village. The sunset bathes the trees in an unearthly glow, lays down an even silence. Half asleep, she walks through beauty she takes for danger, and everything around her feels intangible. Inside the church, black-clad women whitewash the steps, shine the aging wood of the pews, and prepare to decorate the epitaph. There's incense in the air, and the dead have risen and sit at the cantor's psaltery, overseeing the living. No one pays attention to the woman, the black-clad women sparing her not a single look. Only their grandchildren, plump and freshly bathed, holding apples and roses in their hands, squat down in their lust to look up her dappled dress. "Grandma! This one's peed herself!" shouts the fattest child, his voice sounding distorted, rippling, almost singsong. The crone approaches the woman. "And where did you come from?" she asks. "The city." "What city? Doesn't it have a name?" "The city."

Then the church lights go out. Doors are bolted shut, heavy keys turn in locks, the streets empty. The old women return to their homes and light a fire, roasting potatoes and quinces, cats curled safe at their feet. Children blow at the coals and watch them change shape, take on the forms of demons and ancient beasts who blink red eyelids and unfurl razor-sharp tongues. The cold seeps through the windows, settles over the black and white photographs, thickens into a rime of memory. At the kafenio, the smoke gathers against the ceiling, the laughter is thunderous and breaths reek of alcohol. The clock's hands move in accordance with a procession of carafes of wine. There's no worry. No pain. Inside the church, the dead are alone in not contemplating their land. They talk among themselves and don't care if there are trees or utility poles or sidewalks outside. Besides, the Virgin Mary in her blue stained-glass window distorts the view.

You'd think the night is endless, you'd think it hides within it all the years passed and all those to come. Yet in those hours till dawn, the woman will make it to some flowering meadow and give birth to the children she did not lose on the road. She'll give birth. Six sickly children and perhaps a healthy one. The birth: red marks on the grass. A little to the side, the wild cries of animals, lambs slaughtered for tradition's sake, their brains spilling on the ground. Her babies lie by fur skins they pull over themselves, looking now like newborn animals that in moments grow up to become boys of seven or eight. Merry children with two heads or three legs, no eyes, antennae, crest-like bumps on their skulls. Carefree, picking bloodstained daisies and laughing.

And so, on Good Friday afternoon, a hard rain falling on their heads, the villagers all hold bloody flowers in their hands. Inside the epitaph, the woman sleeps, sheltered from the rain and the wind. Her children lead the crowd down cobblestone alleys and forks in the road, over bridges and through squares. They parade their mother around, carrying a harmony that was not bequeathed them, the magi of a vicious ritual. And the villagers follow in a trance feeling a kinship of some other land. When night falls, they ask the woman to dine with them on Holy Saturday, and she declines no invitation.

All Saturday night, the woman goes from house to house, eating and singing alongside the drunken villagers. They tell her legends about the fairies who appear at night in their chapels, promise to lead her through untrodden fields and hidden paths, offer her votives and relics, get her to sit on the most precious spot in the house, the old man's chair, the old man who'd raised fifty children and grandchildren and who, when he died, was taken to the cemetery at the head of a procession accompanied by violins and mandolins. When the hour grows late, the woman leads them to their beds and lulls them to sleep. Before she leaves, she hides a small bottle under their pillow as a talisman, a fragrance made of touch refused and shock-induced laughter.

No other Sunday ever dawned like this. Never before was the

sky so generous with its light, nor the air with its scents. Even so high up the mountain, you could feel the sea. Yet the villagers, drugged by the fragrance, drift in their sleep. With their last sigh they leave behind a story belonging to their grandparents, who sowed the land and tended lovingly to their animals, leave behind one exhalation of fresh wind, the sirocco they, the fortunate, inherited. Those villagers who did not die that night were later poisoned by vegetables from their gardens or they froze in the unexpectedly bitter cold that set in, in April. Weeds took over the slopes of the deserted village and spread to the houses. They choked the children who sank beneath their homes' foundations, buried under leaves and blossoms. Those who saw them said they were smeared with dirt, berries, and rain. Within a few days the village was nothing more than a vast meadow, might never have existed, seeing as no one lives here anymore to confirm it did, and as for me, how can you believe my tale, me with my five nostrils and not a single eye.

As soon as summer came, we took the Spring of Cities by the hand and left the village. She was prettier than ever, clad in black with vines tangled in her hair. Migrating birds, we came back to winter and meet again our night in almond-green fluorescent lights and this paralyzed, overflowing silence that falls when you lie in a lover's arms. We were leaving the village behind, all the children, fathers unknown, fathers dead, we, the ugly children, with our serpent tongues, holding Spring by the hand as we walked away, skipping alongside our mother with short, sharp giggles and muffled cries, each step erasing the last—migrants, walking blindly on until the next year, searching for the new beauty we would haunt.

Snow Milk

We live in still waters. A lake, Mother calls it, though I don't know what to tell you. I just look at the window at a view that's always the same. In winter when the lake freezes over, I venture outside and onto its smooth surface. I take one or two uncertain steps, then fall—clumsy as I am—on the flat crystal that reflects the stranger that is my own form. My life is projected through a square of smudged glass. Mother won't let me go to the shed, get a piece of cloth and clean it. She keeps me tied to the wooden chair by the window so I don't miss a moment of that magnificent view. The other night I said to her, "Don't be afraid, Mother. Stop biting down on my arm, I won't go. Stop biting down on me and I'll still love you." And she let go of my arm and took to biting down savagely on her own, yelling, "Is this what you want, then? Is this what you want?" And slowly, almost ritually, I gave her my arm again and felt, suddenly, that I loved my mother even more.

I can't recall how many times I've seen the lake thaw then freeze over again, though I should not be this ungrateful. Mother celebrates my birthday every year by making me a large cake, usually with moldy jam. It doesn't taste that bad, though even if it did, I'd be sad to have to part with Mother for a few hours just so she could go downtown to shop. On this year's birthday she gave me an unexpected gift. It was not yet dawn when she came to my bed and untied the bandages that for years now have bound flat my breasts.

She kissed me tenderly on the forehead, then walked out of the room, leaving me all alone with a new sensation. Mother cares for me, and I know I owe her my very life. Though I said I can't remember exactly how old I am, still, I feel like an infant, barely months old, an infant whose hands and eyes and voracious mouth are searching for its mother's nipple to lull it to sleep.

The truth is, that what family we have left don't understand how well mother cares for me. They accuse her of keeping me locked up in here but what I'd like to know is, can't they see that out the window lies nothing but a vast expanse of frozen lakes? Where could I go in such bitter cold? Mother rejects their company and to me they seem a threat that could so easily upend the peace and order of our lives. A few weeks ago, we were visited by a distant nephew of Mother's who hadn't even finished his tea before he began spouting theory after theory about the error that was my isolation. Mother was as imperturbable as ever but I couldn't take it, I snapped, throwing myself at him and scratching at his face till it bled. He rushed out the door and ran from our house screaming. I watched from the window his mad dash across the frozen lake, how he'd slip, fall, push off with both palms to stand up again, the palms sticking to the ice, leaving behind them small bloody signs of punishment.

From what I've gathered from Mother's tales we live in a town with more than its share of bridges. Small boats come and go stoically on its lakes and all our people's legends are to do with water. Mother won't tell me the town's name, fearing I might someday open the door and go while she sleeps. How silly of her, to not realize I'd never do such a thing, now that I've come to understand how sheltered I am in here. Beyond the lake lies a vast, strange and dangerous world. In this house, I can hear only the snow's silence. And I can see, of course. Through the glass I can see snowflakes fall on the sole tree the frost hasn't yet killed. This time of year it never gets dark near the lake. Even at midnight the sky doesn't turn black, there's just this muted light that falls everywhere, that momentary azure of late afternoon that the rest of the year lasts for only an instant, the moment before the sun sets. Those seconds before the day sets behind the mountains, I've been counting for years, gathering them up in my mind, and I suppose that they're those same seconds the soul needs to leave the body, seconds that vary with the heat and the cold, and the position of the moon over the earth. But now the sun stands forever unmoving at half-mast. Pinned in place. So that, I admit, I sometimes forget all about the passing of days and months—the sky never runs out of watercolor, it's only the snow that washes it out and rarefies it.

When I was little, I used to draw on rectangular sheets of paper but my sketches were always so blank. White, the whole sheet white, and in the middle of it a tree or a small dead animal. I tried to run away once, to get as far from the house as I could in order to see what was behind the glass then draw it on my sheet of paper, so I wouldn't have to look at it so blank. When I came back two days later Mother was waiting for me with a large pair of scissors in her hands and a cold look in her eyes. She pinched my cheek so hard broken little red stars appeared on my skin. In one abrupt motion she cut my hair short, then made me stand on the kitchen table and lifted up my dress. She spread my legs and with a fierce look said "You better not have . . ." then served me my dinner, dust stew, and it was the first time ever I didn't like the food she'd made me. I did love my hair though, so much. And wanted it kept long. Therefore, I should never leave again. I loved Mother too, so much. And wanted her kept close. So I stayed.

From then on, we've slept in the same room. Our beds side by side. I hear her snore, cough and choke in her sleep and wonder how close someone needs to be to you to allow you to live with their sighs and nightmares. I gaze at her sleeping form, watch it grow old. I stay the same. Like the landscape outside our window. The seasons pass over me and leave no mark. It's only those broken stars that grow with time, come of age, my face a bloody canvas. One night I lifted up my dress just as my mother had done and muttered to myself, "You better not have . . ." and then was lost in a small pool of red watercolor. It'd be enough to make people think, "Silly girl . . . Born next to this vast, watery surface and look at her now, drowning in barely five colored drops." I got up from the chair and went to the kitchen. On the windowpane was me, a small, bloodied animal drawn on snow-white paper.

It was only last night that I killed Mother. I didn't mean to. She woke with a start, struggling to breathe. "Don't just stand there," she screamed, "get some water!" and I took the pillow from my bed and held it over her face. Closer to me than ever, more mine than ever, that's what she felt like as I held her down, writhing, sweating, possibly crying. When her chest stopped moving, I stood up shakily and walked out of the house. Using the fire tongs we turn logs over with, I tried for hours to break through the ice, finally managing it a little before dawn. I ached and shivered but more than that what scared me while I broke through the ice was that it seemed I was also breaking my weak eyes' reflection on it. My bloodless, tight lips and sharp cheekbones. I returned home and walked around it wall to wall. Inside Mother's trunk I found a hidden calendar and a large book with all the country's legends. The date told me Christmas was dawning. I'm not so good with time, and know that for me the holiday is nothing more than just another day of muted blue light. I lifted Mother off the bed and took her in my arms. She felt light, still warm. I got out and walked across the cold marble. When I reached the hole, I knelt down and gazed for a moment at Mother, but couldn't recognize her. Maybe this was my punishment. I let her slip from my arms into the water and watched her disappear with her white nightgown floating up to her shoulders. You better not have . . .

Today downtown they'll be celebrating Christmas. Legend has it that the oldest girl in the house dons a white robe and goes out, door to door, humming an old Neapolitan song. I don't know where Naples is, but according to its picture in the book the girls who live there are beautiful. They have ample breasts and have a look in their eyes you'd almost call lustful, though I don't know if they too have mothers. You can't have it all, no one can. In a little while I'll get off my chair and go outside. Where I broke through, the ice will be frozen over and I won't know where my mom is buried. For all I know, she could still be asleep in the bed next to mine. I should have marked the spot. But how? It's just a white sheet of paper with a tree and a dead animal in its middle. I read in the book that at the bottom of the lake lies the city of the dead. Nonsense. If the dead live down there, then who are we, living up here?

Party on the Veranda

And the girl gave birth to her mother.

Everywhere in the maternity ward: people, flowers, embraces.

And the girl gave birth to her mother, who looked like a tiny little thing, a spoonful of velvety cream, an unripe cherry covered in blood. And in the baby's eyes, a familial sadness, that one day, God forbid, would become the cause of sorrow.

And the girl took the baby in her arms and whispered to it, "And now, Mother, you will live as though nothing were your fault, as though it were all my doing. This too is a burden. Lighter than responsibility, but a burden nevertheless."

And the baby, out of place in this new, white world, would open its eyes to the ladies in white that bathed, nurtured it, laid it down on creaseless sheets, held it in their arms, their faces expressionless, as though removing a chicken from a shopping bag and burying it in the snow inside the freezer. And while the girl packed her things into a suitcase, she would talk to the child. An old habit of mothers, to mumble while doing the housework, as though talking to an imaginary friend who kept them company while they swept or comforted them as they struggled to get a tough stain off an old doily, an heirloom belonging to their grandmother.

And the girl's words, incongruous for her age, poured out riverlike:

"You will be five when you pee your pants during the school play. Terrified, down there in the audience, I'll want to curl up and die. On the way home you'll get an almighty slap to teach you never to do that again. You'll get a bloody mouth, and suck on the blood all the way home. Through open windows, you'll hear laughter and music. There'll be wonderful summers in the city.

"You'll have trouble learning the alphabet. You'll learn one letter every year: fun, farm, face, field, fuck. If you use words like that too often, I'll get a big bar of soap and wash out your mouth. If you're a good, well-behaved girl, once a week I'll get you a large ice cream. You'll suppose it might be worth staying so deafeningly quiet, so long as it's pistachio.

"Sunday afternoons you'll do your homework for Monday. From then on, the word *melancholy* will forever be synonymous with Sunday.

"At school you'll be taught folk songs. Every day you'll memorize another metaphor for death: He'll talk only in rhyming verse. He'll be dressed in black. He'll come across you once in a dream that, who knows, might be a vision. There'll be a series of questions and answers. Your feet will already have begun transforming into some climbing plant. You'll have short stories taught to you. About drownings at sea and the black-clad, many-blighted herald that is the fate of women. The mood will be romantic and mournful. Then recitations, bombastic and rhythmical. Getting hit with a ruler.

"As you grow up the house will grow smaller. I'll wipe the table frantically before your every meal, and every room will smell of disinfectant. I'll get older and older. You won't be able to put up with me for too long. You'll forever remain a teenager.

"Then, the walls of old age: white and blinding. In the living room, untouched by time, a bygone air will persist. Plastic dolls and plant stands; porcelain animals and blue Chinese vases; fake roses, their velvet worn. In the kitchen, electrical appliances spotted with rust, yogurt cups dropped under cupboards and forgotten, broken mosaic tiles. The further away you drift, the more my desire for order will diminish. I'll die in filth, emaciated and incontinent."

The girl folded the last of her clothes and zipped the suitcase shut.

Took her mother in her arms and left the maternity ward before she found the time to whisper in her ear a lullaby or two about falling in love. After all, she couldn't even begin to imagine the baby might ever be hurt inside a body that screamed love.

They came home to a great welcoming feast, a party out on the veranda. Doors wide open, neighbors coming and going, best wishes raining down. An urban summer in '62, with lemonade and Jello, fondant and vermouth and dog-shaped cookies and colorful little flags and meatballs pierced with toothpick umbrellas. The kind of party nobody throws anymore, all those aunts walking in with their platters and pots of steaming food, hurrying about with their hair caught in tight, firm buns, setting tables with dishes whose recipes they'd never give away. Scattered throughout the house, children in their Sunday best—navy shorts and sandals—running wild, dragged-down tablecloths and knocked-over glasses trailing in their wake. Stern mothers chasing after them, giving them thunderous looks, then sitting them down on their laps, wringing out their boundless energy, quenching their inner fires.

"Go on, my boy, recite that poem you memorized for your school's year-end celebration, the one you recite so well! Wait till you hear him! Just imagine, his teacher asked to see me a couple of months ago, 'Ma'am,' she told me, 'your son is great at everything. A child must have it in him, but it's down to the family too . . .'"

The boy stands up, bored, recites the poem loudly if somewhat hurriedly while tugging at his trousers:

In the mountains gleaming clouds
thunder over dome and nave,
darkening a sky too-loud,
stir again a fearful wave.
The young sailor sings his song,
flattening his unreefed sail:
"Greek my mother, Greek her son,
Clouds for naught, I do not quail!"
Wave by wave he's tossed and swallowed

sailor's grave the black seas hollowed
Still the sailor sings his song
in the throes of storm and sea
"Greek my mother, Greek her son,
Lord and Maker, He keeps me!"[1]

"Bravo, bravo!" his grandmother cheers. "Mark my words, one day this boy will be in the papers! He'll be bigger than Princess Sofia's Carlos!"

Platters emptied, cakes melted, steaming coffee served in the sitting room, streetlights on, the men chattering away couldn't care less about the royal wedding:

"Business is booming, we've got a bunch of construction projects in the works. The economy's growing, finally we'll catch a break too! We'll be like Europe! Did you get a load of those apartment buildings? Next thing you know it won't be embarrassing to say 'Greek'!"

Coffee cups are drained, eyelids grow heavy, the hosts make it clear it's getting late, the guests take their leave a few at a time.

"We should go too, shouldn't outstay our welcome, besides, we've got tickets to go see Bithikotsis at the Park. Everyone's saying *Beautiful City* is a dream of a show, it's such a shame you couldn't come."

The veranda clears of people, the kitchen grows quiet, dew has fallen over rooftops and clotheslines, a last few guests have stayed behind, chatting in the hallway.

It's been a while since the girl locked herself in the bathroom. No one's come looking for her. Seated on the toilet, she's having soufflé that's grown cold. A piece of cake too. She's left the tap on so no one will hear her crying. How she'd love to be out there. But no, she wouldn't enjoy herself in their company. The girl wants to go to the Metropolitan to see Hatzidakis.

---

1. Georgios Vizyinos, *The Poems*, vol. II, (Athens: Idryma Ourani, 2003), translation in this volume by Kostas Kaltsas.

In the north bedroom, the most secluded room in the house, sleeps the mother. A baby wedged in between gifts and flowers, swaddled in pink sheets and white pillows and powders and perfumes. The girl, immature bride that she is, knows her mother is locked away in some corner, grounded, yet can't crawl to her because her little legs are as soft as pastafrola dough, her toes like melted birthday candles. Nor can she call out, though if she could, she'd only scream "Fire!" Set fire to the onesies and the dowry, let the fire burn among the crystals and the rattles.

The last of the guests leave with their Tupperware full of leftovers. The girl wipes cake off her lips, unlocks the bathroom door, enters the bedroom, and takes the baby in her arms. Carries her out to the veranda. The girl doesn't know what to say to the baby, who is slowly opening its eyes, whimpering with hunger. The girl doesn't know what to say so she just undoes her robe and starts feeding it.

Who knows, maybe they'll be alright after all.

So, the girl who gave birth to her mother, her child in her arms, sits now in a wrought iron chair, girl and mother pierced alike by the June night. In the strange summer of '62, in this embryonic Athens, unaccustomed to its own bright lights, trying in turn to soothe, to dandle—if it can—the wilderness it inherited.

The Black Box

The noise in the distance sounded like a lawnmower breaking down. But there are no houses with gardens nearby. The area is coastal.

The coastline that delineates his town must of course come to an end somewhere. Eventually. Its borders stillborn. But he'll never know. When the frayed string he holds on to is stretched taut, that's when it's time for him to go home. He sets off on his walk at seven in the morning, the streetlights still on and the fog, that viscous vapor, property of the city, blurs every shape. He's been advised to walk, and so every day he puts on his small, almost child-sized brown boots and carves out his very own labyrinth in the sand. Turning his mouth to the sea, he wonders if, when he can no longer remember which way to go, when he's crawling along the shore using only his eyes, someone will be there to pick him up and take him in their arms and guide his light body into the deepest embrace.

Nothing else can reassure him but this vast beach where memory empties without remorse. He imagines that once upon a time, during the ceasefires of some long war, porcelain ladies holding parasols strolled along the shore, ready for their first swim. They'd have lace detailing on their toes and corsets made of coral and mother-of-pearl. All around them would unfold an entire world of half-naked blond children and dogs running wild between the legs of plump governesses, a world of lemonade vendors and varicolored grandmothers in silk robes soaking in the ocean shallows. He imagines, too, sad poets renouncing the carelessness of time and, buttoned up tight in their beige suits, reading newspaper headlines about the army's victories and transmuting them into bloody refractions in the water. Summers of war, the weather dull, drizzling its days into the sea, leaving its small wet stains on all-white dresses.

Today, though, the fog has descended almost to the sharp tips of the rocks, and over his head fly civilian aircraft that carry on their wings hopes and maps for departure. It's those few moments before he returns from his walk that allow him to recreate the most trivial of details and events. He may not be able to recall if this morning he ate buttered toast or fruit, but he can describe, fairly accurately, his wife's New Year's Eve dress from twenty years ago: green velvet with a boutonniere pinned to the left breast. Her face appears faint to him now. He sees her laughing without sound—howling with laughter, beckoning him close, but he can't speak to her, and her figure fades away inside a house festively decorated with lights and plastic mistletoe.

The deterioration of his speech was inevitable. It's not so much that he mixes up syllables and words, as that he can't recall the meaning of phrases and how to connect them into sentences. So, he avoids interacting with other people. He chose this very beach for his daily walk because it's almost always deserted, because he's afraid that if someone suddenly stops him to ask the time or the way to the train station, nothing will come out of his mouth but the drawn-out cry of a seagull. He thinks seagulls must feel sorrow on still days since they won't be able to find food. Rough seas mean fish coming to the surface and remaining there while the gulls' heads attack the water and snatch them to feed their young. The fish remember, and this is why they remain near the surface. And even if they don't remember, they surely know because it's encoded in their body that this repeated image of birds diving into the water is their own safe story too. No agony. No pain. And so, on still days, the gulls fly sadly to the shore and tear each other apart. The man sees in his mind's eye the image of a vast bloody shore, a watery abattoir of broken eggs and the small white feathers of innocence. Thankfully, this image too quickly fades.

Despite the treatment he was given, these images fade as quickly as words do. He doesn't believe it does him any good. The white little memory pills don't seem to him any different than the candies he ate as a child—his course can't be reversed. The only thing that saddens him deeply is his inability to tell a complete story. He knows that things aren't just the words that name them, they're also their own density, but this gives little comfort. It will be years before the code of human communication changes, but there will come a time when syllables are replaced by energies, and maybe then we'll truly become part of the universe to which, so far, we've been done the favor of belonging. At this thought, the man smiles imperceptibly, the moon slowly fades in the sky, and out of its outline is born the day.

Inside the plane making its way to the capital, a passenger feels as though the clouds are immense pillows soaked with injections that quench pain. He keeps his eyes open and can't fall asleep because he imagines he's lying inside the fluffy belly of a swallow, where it's too hot for sleep. He loosens his seatbelt and looks out the window. They're flying over some city, but the fog is awful, and everything's grey and a little brown, the sea looks like sand and the sand like stagnant water. He sees himself wading along the beach, picking up small shells with no living organisms inside. The woman in the seat next to him moves in her sleep and her blanket slips off, revealing her belly and hands. He thinks of her alongside him on this endless walk, like a small seal following behind him, barking out high-pitched cries. Her skin glossy and shiny, she's now free of the weight of her legs, and it takes little effort for her to drag her flippers across the sand. They'll meet again in the next life—it hardly matters what species we will all be reincarnated as. The small wounds of this older world will remain as signs by which to know each other. Some will have healed, albeit imperfectly. So, though the woman will crawl on her fins in the sand, her eyes will always be blue. Her eyes, lakes.

They were flying back together from far away. The operation had failed yet again. The doctors had said her legs were paralyzed from the waist down, and this type of operation is not just difficult but extremely risky. The man suggested that he wear a sling, carry her with him everywhere. The doctors laughed for as long as they were allowed to and said, "Don't worry, medicine advances with every passing second, advances even at night, while you sleep—we don't lose hope." "We don't sleep at night," the man said, wheeling the metal chair out of the room. The hospital corridor became a square where he pushed his five-year-old along in a pink stroller piled with crochet animals, dolphins and eagles.

If only you could have been born together, erase all that lost time. Start the story together. Choose the story. So, the man is now her father. A strange, melancholy father of thirty-five. His body healthy, hers atrophying from the waist down. From the waist up, wildflowers grow with extraordinary speed, reaching up to her eyes. Piercing the blue, leaving behind them an afternoon refraction on two lakes.

It happened unexpectedly. They used to go on long outings, never choosing big cities, they loved canyons and rivers. They'd just climbed up a rough path and reached the mountaintop. Snow everywhere around them, but despite this soft layer covering everything they could see, peeking out from behind bare tree trunks, small animals and strange insects—metallic, silvery beetles like precious jewels embedded in fairest skin. All around them nature was celebrating her beauty the way the elderly celebrate their birthdays: with humility, wisdom, and gratitude. They could have lain there in the vast white, and morning would have found them frozen stiff, marbled kings in the capital's main square, dressed in their expeditionary garb. It would have been over faster. But the woman simply fell. Fell slowly. When her knees touched the ground, the sound was sweet, nothing that would disturb such silence. The scene like a Japanese painting. A horizon at sunset, snowflakes in her hair, skin made of crystal. Through her skin gleamed small flowers, water lilies, and jasmine. If one were careful, it would be possible to break the crystal with a hammer and chisel, spirit away those winter flowers to somewhere warm. The man ran and lifted her in his arms then over his shoulders as though she were prey, and thus they trundled down the slope, a set of limbs meant for assembly now assembled, until night fell. Stomach on back, lips on neck—strange how certain rugged paths, miles away from home, bind people to each other. The man reached the plain with a wounded fox across his shoulders, a fox that, caught in a hunter's trap, was too proud to ever make a sound. Its fur rich, its eyes amorous.

It could've happened anywhere, somewhere in the city, in the safe square footage of their kitchen, she could've been holding a Chinese teacup that would have been smashed to pieces when she fell. But this would change nothing. It would still be the beginning of the same story, in a different spacetime continuum, some other dimension.

The sun is almost high in the sky, and the string has stretched taut enough that the man on the beach feels a slight itch in his left palm. Normally he'd be back by now, but there's the distant buzzing in his ears, a lawnmower breaking down, hypnotizing him into eternal stillness.

When he was a boy, he lived in a house with a garden. You wouldn't call his family wealthy, but back then it was common to live in a house surrounded by a lawn. The orange-tree street—that's what their road was called—consisted entirely of identical dwellings, square boxes with tiled roofs and plastic chairs in the garden. If asked now, he'd say that the neighborhood had an old-fashioned air and smelled of peeled orange. They drank orange juice for breakfast, ate oranges after lunch, made orange compotes, and baked orange syrup cakes on birthdays and feast days. Whether a little, unspoken family secret or custom preserved in formaldehyde, what matters is that if you're not going to stick up for your birthplace you are truly unworthy.

On Saturday afternoons when the weather was good, his father would give him the lawnmower and set him upon the lawn. When you're twelve it feels great to be assigned such tasks, meaning as it does that you're considered grown up and responsible. But for the man it wasn't exactly that. He always started off happy, spinning around the garden, carving shapes out of cut and uncut grass, but as time went on, he was seized by this strange dread that made his limbs freeze in place. What would happen if, in a moment of carelessness, he lost control of the machine or accidentally pressed the high-speed button and the thing went mad? How would it play out if it flipped over and caught his foot? Or his shoelace? He imagined himself being crushed by the lawnmower's sharp teeth, dismembered, sucked into the machine, fading out of consciousness with the taste of freshly cut grass in his mouth. Really, where does the grass go when it's cut? And where do orange peels go when you drop them inside the garbage disposal?

So he always left the grass half-mowed, though no one scolded him for it, nor thought of sparing him this torment, repeated unchanging every time, a habit in every house on Orange Street that weighed every Saturday down with this violent rite of passage into adulthood. The man walks along the shore and thinks there must surely be a place where the peels of citrus trees and the damp lawns of childhood can come to rest. Someplace next to Heaven. The image puts his mind at ease, but the buzzing comes back louder, more aggressive, more voracious.

And the plane is falling from the sky. It should only take a few minutes but time is a little lump of blue plasticine. You can mold it so that it looks like a small marble or spread it all over the floor, the thinnest layer of spilled detergent. The announcements were made a while ago, hoarse at first but reassuring. Then the voice began to surrender, you can always tell a voice without faith, it sounds like dry, barren land. Now it was time for the pilot to emerge from his cramped little room. God reaching out to his flock. A well-dressed city god who broke his watch and missed all his appointments. The man is unperturbed. He's painted a door on the carpet and shut himself away in his hatch. They sound distant to him—the voices of grown-ups, the clink of dishes washed in the sink. He knew this plan would work one day. The woman next to him hasn't awakened, she's on powerful sedatives for the pain that keep her under, pink pills, fourth generation, a generation nervous and angry. The man wasn't able to figure out whether both propellers had failed or the engine or whether the plane simply tired and surrendered with a sigh. Not knowing is better. Better to have your mind go blank, your head lighten, better to climb the sky more painlessly. To fly.

The shapes beside him are slowly dissolving through a grey haze, the toy disassembles, you can see its insides, its multiple carcinomas, the sound of a lawnmower breaking down is not the sound of a motor but the sound of wails, wails of grief and cries for mercy, and the painting being made is not Japanese, not pared-down, for the faces have sagged and tissue is showing through the skin, and limbs are beating violently against the seats and windows, and flesh is melting away leaving behind nothing but bones like spikes, and limbs turn into insect legs crawling to the roof, and they are praying mantises eating their mates to keep them from seeing, and the Pure Mother has forgotten all about them, is handing out milk and flatbreads made of wheat in a Mexican soup kitchen, and the babies are crawling and touching each other, and the women's wedding bands have rolled down the aisle, a bad sign, and the flight attendants have become ordinary, ugly figures, their lipstick melted and their backs soaked with sweat, and everyone is calling everyone else by their first name, just when did they find the time to get to know each other and become relatives and mourn their brothers, their sisters, and their children, and the books have fallen open on some dog-eared page, and their hands are seeking out good luck charms, and official-looking orange vests are handed out, and it would be better for everyone were they to crash into a landscape snowed white, but this isn't to be because the city that spreads below is an industrial one that lives and breathes and heats milk in small pans and gets dressed to go to work, and the smokestacks of its factories are getting closer and closer, and they all see clearly now the coast and the sea that looks like sand and the sand that looks like stagnant water.

The woman is still asleep in her seat, and there are no voices to wake her because the passengers have settled and curled up in their seats. An immense silence that turns inward and becomes prayer. The world disintegrates, leaving behind only faint sketches: here's where the sea will begin, deep blue for night; the leaves will turn to fertilizer; the animals will hibernate in winter, they'll dream. Not a single human being anywhere. The forms surrounding the man are now faint colors that evaporate until finally all that remains are smells. He shuts his eyes and kisses the woman's legs, lips on buttocks, the sketches predicted something for us, too, but we didn't abide by it. He kisses her with a passion made reckless by their circumstance, puts his hand low on her abdomen but quickly draws back for fear of waking her. He would've liked to let it rest there for a while. He feels certain she sees him clearly in her sleep, explaining to her in some future language how deeply he loves her, she sees him clear as can be, waving goodbye.

Now a thick brume invades from all around, they're surrounded by the clouds of their adolescence, they swallow them, it turns out it was true they taste like cotton candy and cherry ice cream; they'll meet again in the next life.

And the plane crashed on the beach at the man's feet, a wounded swallow made of steel.

What matters isn't whether you can tell a story. There are always sources for the evidence of place and time; there are photographs, events survive, are self-existing. And there's always the black box that holds captive inside it the plane's exact course from takeoff to landing and is the only thing that survives a crash.

What matters is that you've lived a story.

The man traces his route backwards, wrapping the string around his wrist. No doubt by the time he gets home he won't be able to recall or describe exactly what happened, but he doesn't mind. He'll be scolded for being late, then with excessive, irrational care they'll make him his lunch. He shakes the sand off his boots, enters the house, and climbs the stairs to his bedroom. He takes off his shirt, looks at himself in the mirror in his white undershirt. A wild river spreads from his eyes to his left cheek that will swell on winter nights, a deep canyon of a mouth.

In the dining room, voices and laughter signal the start of lunch and invite him to join in.

Quietly, the man descends the wooden staircase.

From that moment on, he'll never speak again.

Rooster with Pasta

He hunched across the wide avenue. By the time the green light flicked on, his head was already down by his knees. In everyone's memories he's tall and proud. No one would ever think of him as stocky, of course, or as one of those men built for heavy lifting, a tinkerer at home. He had a sadness about him and always looked like a fifteen-year-old, weak-bodied and dark-skinned, legs crooked and bruised. His peers describe him sliding down mountain slopes, ripping his pants. No one knows how he found himself in the city, tripping over barricades.

He was dragging along a bundle of old sports newspapers and held in his hand a half-eaten loukoumi. He'd been walking for months. The moment he'd been told he was going to die, he'd taken upon himself to make his way back to the house where he grew up, constructing a roadmap from memory. Branching neurons for roads, hematomas for lakes, epithalami for the small cafés of his adolescence, and cells for tiny people—often children or even former loves—who as the end drew near, would shrink and lose their color. The process of apoptosis was known to him: cells become infected, cease to divide, and kill themselves. His people kill themselves.

The houses he comes across are not in their proper place, the trees have vanished from the sidewalks, the posters on various walls alternate rapidly, and when he turns at the end of a street expecting to find the old tobacco factory, he's stunned to find instead an empty lot or the entrance to a vast underground garage. Signs fade before his eyes, potholes open up and swallow him down into the city's bowels, and yet he refuses to make peace with the idea that the end of the road might not be exactly what he expects. "Things don't disappear." he always said, "They transform into something different but always remain recognizable. In dreams, you can move through an unfamiliar building, yet you know that it's just a mask for your old school or your first apartment downtown." Behind the mask—a few torn notebooks, cigarettes stubbed out in plant pots, the odd kiss or two.

So, this gentle man goes on believing that upon reaching the end of the road he will be reunited not just with the buildings but with his people too. Energies entangled across the universe, bodies that were tightly joined but were lost in murmurs of selfishness or betrayal, will meet again someday in another place, wearing different faces, and their story will begin anew. And that's his religion, and his science, and his only joy.

It's afternoon when he reaches a square, jostling through the celebrating crowds, a visitor to some great fair. Around him dozens of vendors and amusement park rides and bands playing into mics and the smell of popcorn and pumpkin seeds. Half-lost he decides to enter the house of horrors. He always steered clear of it as a kid, and the other kids his age made fun of him for it, but how could he ever explain to them that his fear had nothing to do with the ghost stories they told each other hanging out in abandoned construction sites at midnight? The feeling that possessed him was the deep horror triggered by those crude figures you came across in that dark little house, the sick laughter that rang out every time your fear made you stumble, the wild, cruel fun those paper mouths had with your fall, opening and closing, opening and closing.

Yet here he is, standing in line, ready to hand over the two tokens required for admission. Waiting in line with him are several parents with their kids, while, if his eyes don't deceive him, somewhere back there he can pick out a former soccer player he'd idolized in childhood whose likeness was to be found on the stickers he'd collected. He looks old now. He's got a small potbelly and is holding on tightly to his grandchild, who might not know the first thing about soccer.

The man's turn comes. Now inside the foundation of his fear, to his surprise he finds his gait is steady, as though he's walking down a wide tree-lined sidewalk. The funhouse mirrors make not the slightest impression, and the figures waiting behind the sharp turns don't look like those he can recall. They're just figures in spacesuits, glass-eyed, their speech is unintelligible, their mouths and ultrasophisticated guns shoot water that, with the help of lights blue and green, make it look like X-rays you have to weave through. Overhead, enormous, infected insects, hairy-textured spiders drop occasionally from the ceiling, making the little children scream. It occurs to the man that even terror is transformed: Nowadays it comes from the future, our existence threatened by deadly radiation, mutated fauna, hybrid flora.

His fear's path comes to an end, and the man goes out into the world again. Nothing is the same as before. The fair has packed up, and what had been a throng of fairgoers is now a gigantic crowd roaring in anger and holding up large banners. He's been caught up in a general strike organized by the sailors. They're all in period clothing, some are roping along enormous lighthouses while other have slung decomposing whales over their backs. Behind the hawkers' stalls, in the midst of all those muscular shipworkers, sit a few elderly captains who look nothing like those stately figures who stoically puff on their pipes and spin yarns of old. These are tiny, invertebrate captains, who lost their shells when shipwrecked and with it their voices, who let out a cetacean scream when the sea was sold, then nothing. Now they sit still, scraping the rust off the iron tables with their fingernails.

People jostle and trample, and the man breaks into a sweat, runs away, heart exploding in his chest, his brain a lake—ready to drown him. The route inside his head is constantly changing, reality no longer has an exit he can reach. He stumbles into shop windows, and they become mirrors that lead him to the other side of the city. The man bursts into tears. Under the canopies and sheltering in sewers, thousands of people are huddled together. Thousands dressed in black rags. The handicapped, pickpockets,

Siamese twins, child prodigies, beggars. At a street corner, a woman with no hair balances an empty sparrow's nest on her head. The man approaches her to hand over his only coin and remaining loukoumi, now a shapeless molten mass in its napkin. The woman grabs his hand and launches into delirious whispers:

"The nest was full of birds. I loved them. Except, they didn't know my head was nothing but a round, frozen planet. No life could grow on it. What would they eat? I loved those birds until they started to give me sores, at night, pecking at my skin, looking for food. Eventually they'd manage to find something, tugging persistently at the neurons of my memory, mistaken for little sandworms. This was how they ate their fill.

"It was I who killed the birds. And it's my own business that I'll now walk the highways with a bare, bony skull.

"It was I who smothered the birds. And woe to me who knew the magic of their song."

The man pulls his hand away because the woman's eyes are full of rage, and he's picturing the birds—small bodies on a surgical table. He wonders, are they cold, wherever they've gone to?

Cars on a track to horror, he's overtaken by every color in the world map of humanity, the traffic lights flash blue and purple, his loved ones flash blue and purple in his mind, he's searching for a pharmacy open for all eternity—seized by panic he'd managed to lose his pills, and all the pharmacies are full of the wounded: soldiers in civilian clothes, kings who barely escaped the pyre, teachers infected during experiments their own students ran on them, lame horses, babies abandoned in jars.

The man faints.

New light has dawned when he comes to, and in the heat, his mouth is dry. He gets up stiffly and walks to the nearest garbage bin. He has to wait in line, a long, pulsating, seething line. When it's his turn, the only thing left is a carton of strawberry-flavored milk. It feels as refreshing as an oasis in heaven. He counts backwards as he walks. The map has now been erased, his brain is a whole roasted nut. He counts backwards as he walks. And this is the one and only truth, that in the end, life reveals that its wholeness is nothing but a dream. A barrage of instincts and impulses, rage and orgasmic joy, spasms of motion and promises of now and forever, a barrage of ecstatic dances and prayers for relief from pain. And of course, love.

He stands now in a clean shirt with a light sweater draped over his shoulders, in front of an iron courtyard gate. Before he can push it open, a woman appears at the front door of the house, laughing and happy, an apron tied around her waist. The house is full of people, there's songs on the radio, the smell of familiar food in the air. They've all gathered to say goodbye to him, but no one gives it away. They're all so happy, after all. As always, his parents are sitting out in the small yard behind the kitchen, where it's cool—his mother is not all in black—and they're all whispering conspiratorially about something unimportant. As they always did. Talked with great solemnity about matters that seemed in their children's eyes terribly complex, so that the children could never understand if their family was living through some actual ordeal or not. "There's my good boy," his mother says, offering him a dried fig tucked away in her robe pocket for twenty years. "There's that boy of mine."

The woman in the apron sets the table, and breezing by before she reenters the kitchen and its hell of steaming pots, gets up on her toes and plants a kiss on his lips. His brothers are playing cards and talking politics with their children sitting at their feet building a universe of rockets and tractors. His eternally unwed cousin dusts off an old photograph next to the mirror and daydreams about living in those times, when it was expected you made it to your wedding night chaste, and your virginity was the most precious apple. The man strokes her hair, pays her a compliment that shakes her to her core, and sits at the table in his own chair that until now had remained vacant. They've laid out the good china, saved for weddings and celebrations, and as if by magic even the broken saucer that was missing is back in its place. One at a time, the seats around the table are filled.

At five o'clock sharp, the exact moment the clock reminds us it's time for lunch, I come down the stairs. I'm wearing an old-fashioned dress I dug out of the closet but haven't parted with my torn-up ankle boots. I take my assigned seat and struggle to sit up straight, so I decide to put my feet up. Food is served, a giant platter of rooster in tomato sauce served with pasta. The man next to me starts eating, telling his brothers that, "We have Sunday lunch, not because we have to, not because we're hungry, but only to restore the memory of that first Sunday afternoon, our first taste of tomato sauce."

Lunch is at its peak, and the radio is playing an old rebetiko tune that everyone hums as they lick the sauce off the rooster feet. They've had plenty of red wine. The man sees them move slowly before him, smiling and touching, and decides the months he spent walking were but a single day, a day that ended with this sweet afternoon, like childhood.

Wine has stained the tablecloths, spilled over the wood of the rotunda, dripped onto the floor, soaked my socks, finds no escape, gathers into a dry pool on the floor, blood of our blood. As night falls, its level rises. Our little feet splash in it, the children spoon it into their mouths. The man's relatives hug one another, the unwed cousin crosses herself too late, having in her gluttony forgotten to pray, the tiny, framed photos on the small coffee tables fall and float, slowly, lazily, the happy woman's dress is stained despite the apron.

And so, at half-past eight, just before we felt the wine thicken in our stomachs and beneath our eyelids we turned, before my astonished eyes, into an oil-painting, a confused dream. As the wine rose to our mouths, we said our drunken goodbyes and began to swim in a pool of laughter, voices, and music blaring from the radio.

At nine sharp, we went down, along with the cutlery and our silver rings. And the last thing I recall is my father happily sinking, then rising again to the surface, pinned to his chair, holding in his hands a crumpled map, soaked through will all his senses, all his love for us. And he really did deserve a liquid depth, a bottom. For his melancholy, and that kindness in his eyes. His embraces, his words. An endless sea is what he deserved, a sea for our redefinition, our reconnection, a sea for our drowned and our missing.

Video Gaming

He'd been playing it for years in his mind. The setting was a vast, bombed-out city. In a soldier's uniform, he hid behind barricades and dumpsters, prevented from zeroing in on his target by the buzzing of an enormous bee inside his head. In this way, he often shot and killed the wrong enemies.

From the start, the rules were as vague and blurry as the landscape. He didn't know how many lives he had left. He had, in the meantime, executed more than his share of civilians. Eventually he tired of it and decided to wreck the game by messing with its programming. He started jumping off the rooftops of apartment buildings. He would climb up the collapsed stairwells between floors, reach the top, then let himself fall. He'd land on the asphalt below with a heartbreaking sound like the snapping a centuries-old tree. His back would split in two. Then he'd get up, climb the stairs again, fall again, whole stands of trees put to death.

The metallic voice inside the game, that had always guided him, would attempt to get him back on track, reminding him of his goal, which at times was to murder an entire gang in cold blood and at times was to find some hidden code that would make his enemies explode. He heard nothing but the insect's song, like a siren in his head. He'd jump and get up again. This was all that happened and all that would happen and all that will happen, an endless game with no rules for all eternity.

There will come a time when the voice tires. When its electronic signals fail to sync. When it ceases to point the way. Then the man will become a small part of the game's storyline. And from that moment, every time that we—glued at night to our computer screens, new would-be players—press the button to shoot, it will be like we're pressing our finger over his heart. He'll be our gamepad, our screen, and our right hand, setting the course. And our own secret mission will maybe be to save him. But we'll never know because the game was made without rules, and thousands of video gamers are added to its storyline every day, a thousand sleepless midnight children struggling to aim straight, escape fast, hide well, balance on tracks, avoid traps, solve mysteries, and, by dawn, ascend over the city as great heroes.

Because we wanted nothing more than for our three dimensions and shining radiance to one day be revealed in high resolution. For a symphony of electric strings to perform over our neighborhood skies while we sometimes fly and sometimes run until we land on our beds safe, our blanket pulled up to our eyes, and the thread that ties us to the universe a May Day braid around our left wrist.

Cuba, 5 pm

I first saw a photograph of Cuba in a book in elementary school. Our teacher told us it was an open-hearted, diverse country, full of music. She'd forgotten to mention that its streets stink, that dust rises like a cloud at noon, that you breathe in air and, with it, fire. She'd forgotten about the giant cockroaches, the rusty bus seats, the ominous little hotel rooms, and this endless, unbearable heat. She was many years wiser than us. She was a grown-up. She should have told me. That one summer I would travel to Cuba to die.

It could be children, bidding him farewell. Dozens of short-cropped heads, eyes half-closed in the morning light. They could sing an old song they'd learned for the occasion. Tall boys in white shirts, lined up on the anniversary beneath a strange, sad sky.

But we're too far away, and it's already too late in the evening for guests. It's almost late. The preserves have melted in their jars, turned to masses of mud, the water in our glasses has turned swampy. Small arthropods float it in now. Soon I will close the wooden door behind me, and the slightest hint of mercy will be extinguished. Outside, the afternoon is strange, curdled. When we were kids, we used to say that it only got dark when the big lights by the highway come on, but here, evening begins indoors, with the walls of our room turning blue, and the light slipping from our eyes, their color dripping onto the concrete floor where it pools in a large stain of visual memory. A calm languor spreads across his face. "Are you afraid?" I ask. "I'm sad," I hear him whisper back.

I hadn't seen him in years. The last time was at a lecture on suicide in poetry and fiction. I sat near one end of the classroom, studying him. I knew full well he would have spent entire nights reading and organizing everything he said that day. And I wasn't listening to him. I was counting the wrinkles on the back of his hands. He held the pen easily and spoke calmly. A slight irony to everything he said, an ambiguity in his expressions, an arbitrary playfulness. With bated breath, the spectators partook in a strange melding, hypnotized into complicity. I was just twenty-five years old.

Now the room is hot. The scorpion sleeps on his right shoulder, keeping him alive. It's summer and the white curtains hang still, languid. His eyes search out my mouth, he's waiting for me to speak, but every morning, every evening, I sterilize my sentences, and the gaps between my words are flooded with this soap whose scent will forever be that of inevitable memory. The mattress that hugs his body sweats in its effort to make him comfortable, take away his pain. He wakes just before sunset. I spoon-feed him ice cream, love him the way one loves little children. I recite for him as many poems as I can recall, then TV spots, recipes for refreshing salads. Then sleep takes him away again.

News of his illness made the papers. Then silence. Soon, I learned his class was assigned some other philologist with stubby fingers and a pursed mouth. The students revolted. Then he became a child. He gave up trying. Climbed back up to his tree house and refused to take the cough syrup, even though it was cherry-flavored. At night he would wet himself. Suddenly, the years separating us had been wiped out.

February, birth month, I met him in a white bedroom. In one bed among many. Like everyone else, he was an exhibit in an ice museum very far from here. He could've been anyone, but I recognized him, for he was the thinnest, the most naked. All of them in the same motionless pose, head tilted slightly to the left and up. He wore no clothes. And I couldn't tell whether there were arms and a chest under the sheet that seemed almost glued-on, a sheet of heavy iron. And if there were, whether they were still in place. Or whether the left leg had become a vertebra or a palm the skin of his heart. He had not a single belonging of his own. He wore five brown bruises on his chest and a plastic tube. It occurred to me that in his sleep he must think himself dead because he had nothing familiar beside him. Not his glass of wine, nor one of his books, nor could he see a TV flickering in the distance, even if the signal in these clinics was always staticky. All the same, in the evening the nurses would dim that white, blinding white light and put some music on the radio so the patients would feel that night was falling.

Out in my own reality, the hours grew more drawn-out every day. And I could no longer make work appointments or meals at home. He was there, motionless, made one with the ironwork of the bed. And those images of seascapes and landscapes emptied out of my head. And he waited for me. Every day. And for him this was a ritual and a celebration, only he couldn't wear clean clothes, nor cook for me, nor call me and ask me to get the newspapers and coffee. And he was thin, so thin I imagined the doctor lifting him off the bed to turn him on his side, while he hung there with his arms wrapped around himself. I'd never seen pain so thin.

All alone and downcast in this thick, darkly colored time, he cried desperately for help. I talked his sister into consenting. By April, he was already out. I'd managed to make her too believe in the colorful, promising Cuba of my textbook, the scorpion patiently curled in his corner waiting for him.

There are some doctors whose hands are not scented with perfume, whose skin is rough and cracked by the sun. Some few doctors with a sorrow that freezes the cheeks at night, doctors who live in another world outside our own, who give their bodies to the flames and have their ashes collected in little transparent bottles. Who tame venomous animals and with their butterfly nets catch electric energies in mid-air. For months now, these ashes have sustained but not revived him. The scorpion always prevails until dusk, and the spider in her shape makes up the ground she's lost at night. She's reached his neck. Her legs pierce his skin. I lie awake, motionless at the foot of the bed, watching him shrink and drift away from me, his head so far away I cannot reach it, his chest a distance I can't cover, it will be years before I've crossed it, I won't make it in time. I'll grow old. Become his mother. Scold him for his carelessness. My hands will slap his face, then these same hands will hold him close. We'll do his math homework together. His grades will be bad. He'll only read poetry.

We'd never traveled together. I always imagined me driving on an endless highway in the morning, parallel to the sea, and him next to me asleep, slumped on my lap, so close to my belly, curled up inside me. We'd never traveled together. Our most lasting common ground was his house downtown. In a room full of books, with many small lights and lamps throwing strange shadows on the walls, I envied the words walking across his hands. I'd swallow his images, and he'd cover my hands in blood, fill my belly with a strange heat, and I held him so tight that we fell asleep all laughed out, the way children do. I envied his words yet knew that on some nights, the decision was his alone, I was his story, and so let him rest easy in his dreams, tracing circles and borders that carried him always to an elusive world, precious, many miles from our own.

We told each other. We spoke so much it would be years before I had to open my mouth again. And my sound and these strange electric pains I feel on snowy days are his.

It's summer now, and his eyes are open, but he can't see. Eyes the blue of a washed-out sky. I tamed the scorpion, got him on our side with hasty promises of feeding him my limbs and I see him now huddled in his corner, helpless and harmless. Unable to face the spider. Outside it's getting dark. The ice cream has melted and turned to water. Far away, the view from the window endless deafening time, and the radios playing a crystal Ernesto Lecuona chorus, sad as afternoon.

The scorpion. The doctors' irrational oasis. The cult of faith. With the scorpion on his right shoulder, he neither dies nor lives. He exists, as the dishes on our iron table exist, as the glass with the straw exists on his nightstand. Fifteen years of meaningful absence filled in one brilliant, blind summer. With the same sheets, with the fungi and germs creeping through the door at night. Me in my chair. Preserved. Alive. I forgive him in secret and go in search of the physics and chemistry that transmuted all that heat, the hot plasticity of his hands, into a musculoskeletal system frozen still. Rigid, frightened, and inadequate. My anger floods over. That it can be so simple. That people's hands are lost.

I see him nod at me. His mouth is sticky, its only movement a subtle opening, an attempt to push the pain away from the corners of his lips. I'll never dare to forget. His fingers on the sheet riffle deciduous books, recite the words by heart. Then forget them and birth them again. I say, I love you, love you so much. And his body vertical, in absolute affirmation, I make him whole walking, whole holding me, I look at him stand upright, and it's Sunday night, and I'll see him again in the morning at school.

It could be poets, bidding him farewell. Standing under our window in dark trench coats. Exiles. But just for a little while, let them leave me be. I'll put on my iron gloves and take the scorpion from his shoulder. The light switch will suddenly flip. The room will be plunged into darkness. The scorpion will be desperate for water. Desperately wagging its tail. And he'll have a sweet smile on his lips. He'll stroke my hand, he'll manage it, he'll say, "You got me." Maybe he'll mumble something more. The last things we say before we fall asleep are never remembered. We can't even remember who stopped talking first. Then his lips will close. I'll grow young. I'll be a schoolgirl. Putting pins in the teacher's chair. The one who didn't know. I'll swallow a fistful of words. There, in a neighborhood, centuries away from the sea, with you beside me breaking into a million bits of light on my belly.

And I'll wait. With my teeth in your palms, I'll wait. For the letters to clog the nose, clog the mouth, form an unspeakable story, the true story of your death, while outside, at the window, the poets and children will only lull us to sleep. Summer in Cuba, a tin evening for a roof, the scorpion and the crab will drown together in our mouths.

. . . when one of them . . . happens on his own particular half . . . the two of them . . . are hardly to be induced to leave each other's side for a single moment.[1]

My love.

1. Excerpted from Plato, *Lysis, Symposium, Gorgias*, trans. W. R. M. Lamb (Cambridge, MA: Harvard University Press, 1925), 143.

The Garden

The house is always on the mountain. A gleam of sea, distant and unreachable. Yet, for all the clouds, I could make out your form on the rock, black waterbird, struggling to spread your wings. Bones crumbling, worn down to skin by sunset, draped over your head like a frayed coat, worn down to yourself, a child-bird, old and frail, my beloved.

The end will come, thick-colored, over my eyes, that deep blue you love so much. For months now you've been gone, for months now I've been drinking nothing but sounds, eating nothing but poems. It was an epileptic summer. I saw it beat at the walls, paralyzed, drying its tears in salt pans. I saw it sedated, carried on a stretcher, a beautiful man who decided to die at dawn on August 31st—my husband.

Here, time is defined by the dew on your trees, the mews of the cat that slinks among the flower beds and crops. Every morning, I see you sitting at the stone table, sleepless, ordering the sun to rise, the night to withdraw, the night that puts its rifle to our heads and pulls the trigger. You stare impatiently at the door, waiting for me to appear through it, holding a newborn story swaddled in the pages of the journals that you left me, its paper protection. Still, I disappoint you. For all I manage every night is the difficult labor of giving birth to my mind. Bloodied, the words drowned, parentless children lost in the snow and illiterate.

I'm writing to you with my body laid out on top of yours. Where did the time go, your nails have grown so long, your hair turned into roots and dug into the ground, became one with the flowers and the vegetables? Now here I am, tending to the greenest of gardens.

The end will come one day as one of my howls at five in the morning, driving the nocturnal animals back to their nests and warrens. The weasels and mice will vanish down their burrows, the spiders will cease hunting their prey, and the black moths will die pinned to the light with psychedelic rhomboids and mazes flashing behind their eyes. It will be a deafening howl, the house will crack down to its foundations, and thousands of birds, thousands of children, will pour out of the walls, out of the wooden doors and moth-eaten windows. You'll be among them, somewhere or other. And I have no other alphabet to pay back, no other image to imagine, having already recognized you in a dream being dragged away from my body, the body of my spasms, by swallows and the wild children of late summer, carried away in the beaks of eagles that cover you whole with their black wings and cries.

The house is always on the mountain. My gaze ends where the sea begins.

A Balcony in the Sky

There's an enormous sandlot not too far from here. Somewhere between our house and the Bay of Bengal. At dusk I can walk home, and you don't have to worry about those reds violently passing me by. With my down jacket thrown over my back, sleeves in a rough knot across my chest, I perform my balancing act on the median strip while behind me the colors deepen, the world sinks and blends together, and any hint of salvation slowly fades. Motionless at the window, you watch me coming, and I draw a bead on you so I don't fall. I'm a tiny dot that grows ever larger, turns fleshy and limbed, and at about quarter to eight, comes home, tired and sweaty from playing. You know, around here we play soccer from sunup till sundown. The girls, gathered behind the wire fence, watch and giggle even though they could never take a decent shot at goal themselves. Girls. Dummies. What are you waiting for?

We all wear white t-shirts and at dawn resemble a piece of sky, a view clear and visible only on cloudless days from our north-facing balcony. A faint line on the horizon. Isn't it strange? The only wounds we carry are a few nicks from a fall. Sometimes—I'm telling you this now, not to scare you but just because it happens—my scalp itches something fierce, like the scab of an old, ancient wound. But you say, "Don't pick at your scabs, my child, for the wound will bleed again and never heal." I imagine scratching at it just so in my mind, and the itch goes away. Then I close my eyes and imagine that this crack in my head is a fissure so deep it reaches to my heart, and I lean over it for a better look and fall into my heart. Gathered there are all my classmates, and you, and Grandma, and folks I don't know, even our deaf-horse geography teacher, but you're all silent and sad. And so, I call out, "Denmark. Capital?" And no one answers.

I'm back here, in the comfort of this place, its warmth like snuggling in bed on Christmas. Out the window, a festive drizzle is falling, and you've been up early. I lie in, watching you out of the corner of my eye as you put away my toys and make me a glass of sugar milk, nectar for princes half asleep. I lie in bed in a suspended state of morning dizziness, though I know I must get up, because even before school was out for the holidays, I'd promised you an old story. I'd rather recite for you from our earth science textbook, fill our day with streams and rainfall, reefs, deciduous trees. But it's New Year's Day tomorrow, and I shouldn't be sleeping. And besides, it's why I came back. And besides, I've got nothing more important to do. Here I go:

An endless Saturday afternoon, me waiting for you to come back. The roof of our house is open to the sky, and snow is coming silently down, sneaking under the chairs, hiding from me. You've locked the front door as usual, but you can't lock out the heavens. Don't ask me to tell you whether the house is small as a matchbox or vast as an expanse of water. It's too difficult for me. Fear enlarges space and lengthens my distance from you. I'm cold but stick my hands in my pockets and wait, patiently, for you to get back. For a while now the flakes have been producing strange reflections. Through my eyelids I see you digging into the sky, desperately searching through this immense and lonely universe for my little blue nightlight. I've laid out all my toy cars on the floor and invented a game that will last until the moment you return. I eat my food and little bits of glass land in my drink. I hope I manage to stay awake, for I want to tell you all about school and read you a poem our French teacher gave us. I want so bad for once to be the one who watches you sleep, for me to be the one to watch over you. But that will probably never happen. Because our pillows now float in a frozen lake. You'll probably be late. The season will have passed over my uncovered eyes, and a blizzard will be raging in the kitchen. I'll have learned to scream images of mercy, and my nails have grown long enough for me to make holes in my own skin. Now you're digging through the clouds with your teeth, your own body paralyzed, you pierce the viscous layer of sky with your eyes and reach the sea.

You'll probably be late. The snow blocked all the entrances, and it's fallen in a soft layer over brightly colored sheets. It will be no one's fault. I'll almost be done eating. First my lips will run like water from my face. My mouth will slip to the floor. I'll be humming with my eyes. The whole of me will be but a drop of skin. My hands will slacken and drop the spoon, release their terror and complaint and embrace my body. I'll be a tiny little marble, I'll roll, lose myself inside a crack in the wall. The hair on my forehead drenched in sweat, swirled in ancient forms, circular, repetitive. My pupils will fade away, my eyelids close to protect the final image seen. This will turn transparent, you will turn transparent, there will be nothing left but a flat sheet of frozen sky.

Je voulais, maman gentille,
T'offrir de belles jonquilles
J'ai regardé les boutiques
Mais les prix sont fantastiques
Et je t'offre ce poème
Pour te dire que je t'aime.[1]

---

1. "Fête des Mères" or "Maman," poem by Michel Beau, translation in this volume by Kostas Kaltsas.

I wanted, sweet mother,
To give you beautiful daffodils
I searched the stores
But the prices were out of this world
And so I offer you this poem
To tell you I love you

You'll come home late. And you'll be tired. Your eyes distorted, half-closed. You'll say, "A royal quilt for my child." The veins in your legs split open, you'll be covered in a forest of bloodied branches. I wonder what it would be like if we lived in a ravaged, war-torn land.

What now? Is it time for me to name the longest rivers in the world? No. Now a concrete garden spreads as far as the eye can see. An asphalt, afternoon road. In our white t-shirts, we stick to the still-wet tar, our wings leaving behind a chalk outline to remember us by. Now the garden's full of birds. Freshly bathed, ready for our Sunday stroll, we kick around a golden ball, kick around the sun. You're very far away. Through a window. Motionless. Always waiting, almost patiently. Waiting for sunset, for me to unlock the door with my key and, exhausted, fall asleep in my clothes. Reaching you will take a maze of time. But it's only then you'll rest. Smiling, surrender yourself to the scant light of the room's lamp, your redeemer, at long last consumed by happiness. Mom. My ears were covered with silk cloths to stop the blood from flowing, and so it's with my hands that I hear your sweet voice reach me and imagine you're here, making all us boys and girls fall in line, teaching us game after game, bursting into laughter at the puzzlement in our eyes, and we never even realize where the time goes. Mom. You cannot be in pain. You'll always be taller than me. Stronger. The end of your sorrow must come suddenly one day and land like a trace of dust on the scraps of your evening meal, on the one remaining bite.

New Year's Day has come and gone too many times, and even Christmas has become a strange holiday celebrated only by the sorrowful. I don't know if here is where you live, and it's still hard for me to say whether my feet tread on ground, asphalt, or the sea. I take my cough syrup every four hours, because I'm telling you, it was just that I was cold, that was all. But not so much as a finger smudge upsets the silvery balance reflected on the glass cabinets of your kitchen. And you, at dawn, throw yourself at them with a running start, those cabinets, with your hands covered in strawberry cake and wet, damp earth. Inside the drawers, the calendar angels have hidden the years beneath the good silverware that shines and slashes through the darkness.

I've made a mess of my homework and all I have to tell you lies forgotten. For centuries now I've carried you, have not for a moment set you down. I carry you inside a deep embrace and lull you to sleep at night, your body unweighted by nightmares. I lull you to sleep so that you'll grow up big and strong, a child of heaven devoted to love. I breathe in your smell, and no one will ever, ever know, because it's all whispers, laughter, and pinches, and pureed food in a little silver spoon, and the sounds of animals and the sounds of birds, and rainy mornings through the car window with a bed of leaves on the ground on the way to school, and drool, and blood, and endless, unspeakable beauty.

Alors, au fond de ma tête
J'ai composé pour ta fête
Un tout petit compliment
Et je t'offre ce poème
Pour te dire que je t'aime.[2]

There's a sandlot somewhere in the North Icefield, a ten-minute walk from our house in a land where it never gets dark. Quarter to eight, with the last cartoons of the day on TV and us half asleep on the couch with crumbs clinging to our mouths. Sounds that will never be heard, stars against your windowpane. As for me, a tiny bloody glow that breaks the absolute blue stillness, in my sleep, I think of you and love you.

---

2. "Fête des Mères" or "Maman," poem by Michel Beau, translation in this volume by Kostas Kaltsas.

So, in the depths of my mind
I composed for your celebration
A tiny compliment
And so I offer you this poem
To tell you I love you

My mom.

Now, in Papa Rabbit's warren, all his children are gathered. Among them, a kid goat, keeping safe between its teeth an eerie song of snow.

Acknowledgments

This edition owes its existence to my dear friends Cara Hoffman and Marc Lepson, with whom we walk together in Art but above all—in life.

Heartfelt thanks to Kostas Kaltsas for the respect and care with which he approached my words and for the impeccable cooperation and to Eridanos Publications for their generosity and support.